DAUNTLESS

DAUNTLESS

HELLCAT RELEASED™ BOOK ONE

MICHAEL ANDERLE

DISRUPTIVE IMAGINATION®

LMBPN Publishing
PMB 196, 2540 South Maryland Pkwy
Las Vegas, NV 89109

Version 1.00, May 2022
ebook ISBN: 979-8-88541-299-5
Print ISBN: 979-8-88541-300-8

THE DAUNTLESS TEAM

Thanks to the Beta Readers
Larry Omans, Kelly O'Donnell, Rachel Beckford, John Ashmore

Thanks to the JIT Readers

Wendy L Bonell
Diane L. Smith
Dorothy Lloyd
Christopher Gilliard
Zacc Pelter
Dave Hicks

If I've missed anyone, please let me know!

Editor
The Skyhunter Editing Team

DEDICATION

To Family, Friends and
Those Who Love
to Read.
May We All Enjoy Grace
to Live the Life We Are
Called.

— Michael

Dante Shale stepped onto the platform from the inter-station transport. The lean man in a long, work-stained coat glided noiselessly toward the exit with the grace and deadly strength of a panther on the prowl. Heads turned at his commanding presence, and a wave of whispers swept through the crowd as they recognized him. A handful of comments rose above the sound.

"Hey, isn't that Dante Shale? Holy shit, the rumors about him coming here were true." A glance showed the younger guy's slack-jawed amazement.

"Wow!" a girl marveled while staring at him, starstruck. "I came to visit my auntie in New Tottenham. I didn't expect to see the greatest Marauder *ever* in person."

"I thought he'd be taller."

"How the hell did he pull off some of that crap? A hundred Dirtwalkers on his last run?" The vaguely Cockney accent caught Dante's ear.

"Naw, I heard it was more like thirty, maybe forty at the most."

Dante scanned his surroundings with piercing green eyes. As a Marauder with a legendary reputation his survival depended on constant alertness. Besides his usual enemies, there were always the young wannabes who tried to challenge him to build their names.

A few faces gazed in awe, a promise to fulfill whatever pleasure he could imagine shining in their eyes. Sometimes they were the most treacherous and a thing to be avoided. Mostly the atmosphere was fear-tinged respect as the crowd parted to let him pass.

As he left the boarding area, he heard the muffled computerized announcement: "Shuttle B19 now departing Londonburg. Stand clear of the vessel. Next shuttle ETA is thirteen ten hours."

Standing outside, he studied his surroundings. The sight of Londonburg never failed to amaze him. The tall spires of steel and synthetics, trees and parks, people everywhere going about their daily lives. A whole city floated in space under a transparent crystal dome whose self-contained gravitic field provided air to breathe and everything to sustain life.

Beyond the barrier was the black of space, punctuated by glittering stars and the net of tunnels and space bridges that connected Londonburg to the other floating Atlantica Stations as they orbited above the ruins of Earth.

He flagged an empty taxi pod, flashed his payment card, got in, and gave his destination address. The pod offered various entertainment options: AI-simulated conversation, music, or videos. He chose silence.

About fifteen minutes later, the pod stopped at his destination and deposited Dante at the curb. As the taxi shot away and rejoined the streams of traffic that endlessly filled the highways, Dante faced the towering structure where he had business.

It was essentially a skyscraper, although vaguely pyramid-shaped, the better to maximize the space available to it while retaining the strongest possible construction. The lower wings were the size of a village square. The topmost reaches were more in line with the dimensions of a typical office building.

The people within undoubtedly needed plenty of space, given how vital their operations were to Londonburg's economy and Atlantica in general. They provided increasingly efficient technologies for gathering solar power, the main energy source throughout the lattice of Stations. It was easier to collect the sun's rays when no longer dealing with Earth's atmosphere.

Before Dante could approach the entrance, he spotted a familiar figure leaving the building and walking toward him. It was Ana Souvanatong, a fellow Marauder. She looked as rough as him in her work clothes except for the hot pink scarf loosely draped around her neck. Dark, braided hair swayed in time with her strides. He'd never worked directly with her but had found her company tolerable enough and a competent ally when they'd bumped into one another during a job.

She looked up, and her eyes widened. "Shale? Damn. I wasn't expecting to see you here, of all places."

Dante shrugged. "Yeah, they got in touch and offered me a job. The money sounded too good to pass up. As long as it's not a setup."

Ana shook her head but kept her eyes on his face. "Man, you have some nerve! I heard you sold that last haul to Intra! I take it you've never heard of corporate rivalries?" A quick thumb-jerk indicated the building behind her.

Dante was well aware that Intra was the hated foe of his prospective employer. He figured both companies would engage in a bidding war for his services. Which of them came out on top wasn't his concern, provided they paid well for his work.

The work wasn't something most people *could* do. Even regular Plunderers weren't that common, and the specialized Marauders were a rarer breed still.

It took a particular type of person to brave the hostile wastes that dominated the Earth's surface in search of what their ancestors had left behind. It required discretion and knowledge as well as courage and toughness. Knowing how to identify the best salvage—high value, low density, so half the profits didn't get burned up on the fuel it would take to haul it all back in a massive ship.

When it came to such operations, Dante wasn't personally aware of anyone with more successes under their belt than himself. His payloads had been astonishingly lucrative for a variety of VIP clients. Some said that his expeditions had the power to make or break entire regimes. Firms went bankrupt for the lack of being able to pay him enough to save them. Other clients were able to dominate entire Stations based on the wealth he procured for them.

Furthermore, given all the times he'd fought his way out of seemingly impossible scrapes or pulled through when everyone had written him off as dead, his name commanded a certain intimidation factor. Simply knowing that he was on a given job was enough to scare most other Plunderers away.

"Yeah, whatever. Corporations are always in competition and don't deserve loyalty," he growled. "I'll hear their sales pitch and make up my mind later. I'm too valuable for them to kill me off just for running cargo for Intra that one time."

Ana retorted, "We're freelancers! They can't hold it against us if we want better pay."

"If those rivals get into a bidding war, all the better for us. They hire *me* because I get the job done. My word is my bond. Most of them are smart enough to know that I expect the same honesty in return."

The last man who tried to renege on his deal with Dante Shale hadn't been able to regret it. He was dead so fast that it took him a minute to realize he had a knife through his heart.

As they moved apart, Ana told Dante, "Well, good luck." Dante shrugged. "Yeah. Later."

The sign in front of the building was low to the ground but broad enough to be easily read from either side of the road. Bold lettering identified the headquarters as Slaine Solar Solutions—a company important enough to get away with being abbreviated. When someone mentioned "SSS," almost everyone knew who they meant. They were more than a fixture of business and industry. To some extent, they were a social and cultural institution.

Cormac Slaine himself was a bit of a celebrity, increasingly involved in politics and commerce or so the gossip went. He'd secured an alderman position for himself and wanted to expand his reach still further. Dante had never met him. He'd remedy that shortly, but as he strode toward the tower's front doors, he felt no particular nervousness beyond the usual sense of alertness to anything that might go wrong. Slaine was only a man. Being rich and famous made him no different from anyone else.

At the doors, Dante paused for about one and a half seconds as a tiny blue light atop the entrance flashed, scanning him for irregularities and opening with a low, somehow comforting *swish*. He stepped over the threshold and into the lobby.

The reception area was stunning, befitting a powerful and important company. They wanted to make a good first impression, and Dante supposed that such extravagance would readily woo most people.

The floor tiles were the highest quality synthetic marble, smooth and shiny but with the appearance of deep layers. The smoky black streaks swirled and expanded through the white stone. Atop this lay elaborate rugs in key positions. The six columns arranged around the sides were also marble and trimmed with gold.

There were two long couches upholstered in deep red and gold and end tables to hold view spheres for anyone who might be bored enough to require one while they waited. A small fountain burbled in the corner near the couches.

The reception desk was synthetic wood, as top-of-the-line as everything else, and wrought with intricate carvings on its outward-facing side. Its top was a thin sheet of faux marble.

Behind the desk sat a man who likely served the dual role of receptionist and security guard. He wore a business suit but also had an unobtrusive earpiece. His shaved head, flinty eyes, and muscular frame gave him the look of someone trained to use violence if he had to.

"Hello. Do you have an appointment, sir?" He looked up at Dante without rising from his seat. His demeanor was chilly but polite.

"Dante Shale. Here to see Mr. Slaine." He didn't think it was necessary to say more than that. If the receptionist pressed him, he could. His nature was to seek the simplest, most direct solution, cut straight to business, and not bother with many pleasantries, formalities, or technicalities.

The man arched an eyebrow and Dante *saw* him shift mental gears into a higher state of alert. The Marauder had implied that he knew Slaine was in the building, and he didn't consider it a special privilege or something to be begged for and granted out of generosity.

Which it wasn't. Slaine had personally requested his presence. There was no point in wasting words on the subject.

The receptionist said, "I see," and pretended to scratch his ear. It probably sent a signal through his earpiece to remind the rest of the security team—who were out of sight but surely somewhere nearby—to pay close attention to this particular exchange. "Allow me to rescan you and to double-check our register."

He flashed a handheld scanner at Dante, mimicking what the door device had done a moment ago, then bent over the sphere on his desk, fingers working rapidly, and touched his earpiece again. It probably linked him to the building's entire system. Dante waited with growing impatience but said nothing. If he thought he had good cause to confront the man for stalling, he would.

It only took a few more seconds. The receptionist gave a curt nod, pushed the sphere away, and looked up. "You're all clear, Mr.

Shale. Your biometric data checked out and you do indeed have an appointment. The elevators are at the end of that hallway to your left. Take the last one on the right to the penthouse. I'll clear it for you from here. Once you reach the top floor, you'll have to pass through a security checkpoint, but you shouldn't encounter any problems."

Dante jerked his chin up in a short goodbye. "Thanks." He went straight to the corridor the guard had indicated, which was blocked off by an electro-fiber barricade. It retracted into the wall as he approached, then reasserted itself, humming and crackling from the slight air interference after he'd passed.

The corridor beyond was high-ceilinged and decorated with quality art prints. Men and women in crisp business suits passed to and fro, heading in and out of the chambers that branched off to the sides. There were one or two individuals he was sure were Marauders, albeit dressed up for the occasion. Important things were going on here. He was amid the Londonburg elite.

Dante was momentarily self-conscious of his worn and casual garb but shrugged it off. He didn't care what anyone thought of him. The only consideration worth devoting any thought to was the prospect that some security guard who hadn't got the message would hassle him.

It took a lot to faze him. As he moved down the hall and cast a casual glance into one of the small conference rooms, a man lounging at a table caught his attention sharply enough that he almost missed a step.

It was Ersan Awir. One of the relatively few Plunderers whom Dante considered truly formidable, to the point that he wouldn't have expected to see the man sitting here of all places. Tall, rangy, dark-faced, with huge hands, Ersan looked like someone who demanded that others take him seriously. They did.

Here he was, probably to receive a briefing on a job sponsored by Mr. Slaine and his firm. It drove home the fact of SSS's ever-increasing power.

It also made Dante wonder what was so incredibly vital that Slaine had insisted on speaking to him personally.

He found the elevator without difficulty. After pressing the activation button, it took a second for the front desk guard to clear him. Then he pushed another that would take him to the penthouse. It was a long ride—the lift moved slower than it seemed like it should. Perhaps it was a security precaution in case an unvetted or hostile party seized control, and the bodyguards on the top floor needed extra time to prepare.

After a moment it slowed and stopped. Its doors opened to disclose a tight, antiseptic chamber dominated by two electronic gates, multiple scanners, and a team of four burly men in armor with batons dangling at their sides. At least two of them appeared to have cybernetic modifications. Probably stamina-bolstering implants beneath their clothes.

One had a prosthetic hand, although it could've been simply a newer model of razorfist. Another man, tall and pale, had eyes that couldn't have been natural. They shone too brightly, and the way they moved didn't look right.

The lead guard, a middle-aged man who was probably unmodified, approached with a dour but placid expression on his long face. "Please stand still," he began in a flat monotone. "We need to scan you and check for weapons. If you're cleared, you will go only to assigned, permissible areas. When you reach Mr. Slaine's office, you will do as he or his bodyguard instruct, and if they ask you to leave, you will do so immediately and without hesitation."

"Yeah," Dante grunted. "Sure. Whatever."

They went through the charade of scanning him for the third time. Then the two cyber-bruisers patted him down for armaments or contraband. Normally Dante preferred to be armed, but he knew he wouldn't be able to get away with it in this case, so he'd left his weaponry with the crew.

Finding nothing, they permitted him to pass through both

gates and pointed out the way to Slaine's office. He felt their eyes on him as he went, especially the synthetic ones of the tall, pale guy. Those *felt* different.

The corridor beyond the security checkpoint was as featureless as the alcove that led to it. Other halls branched off to the sides, but Dante stayed on the main one, following the floor lights that brightened via motion detection to point out the way. He didn't doubt that bad things would happen if he tried to bolt into one of the other chambers.

After another bend, the antiseptic hallway ended and opened into a vast suite of rooms that were nothing like what lay next to them. The ceiling rose nearly seven meters to a peak in the center. The walls were primarily broad windows, although someone had activated the shades on three sides. Immediately beyond the hallway lay a carpeted expanse before an informal office, perhaps more like a den. That was Dante's destination. Beyond an internal wall lay what he assumed were Slaine's living quarters.

"Mr. Shale," a voice intoned, projecting in a way that filled the penthouse, even though its owner hadn't spoken too loudly. "Please, make yourself comfortable."

Dante eyed the two men at the real, not synthetic, mahogany desk that dominated the office area. Sitting behind it was Cormac Slaine. It couldn't be anyone else. His voice was a medium pitch, smooth and pleasant as befitted a man in his position. His appearance was oddly nondescript—a generically handsome middle-aged man dressed in finery, inoffensive in every respect.

Standing next to the desk was an individual who couldn't be any more different. The hulking brute's cybernetic modifications were both extensive and obvious. He made no effort to hide them. Dante had never met the man, but he knew who he was—Eduardo H. Curtidor, former Reaper, known previously as Mr.

Hydraulic. These days, everyone referred to him as Mr. Hyde. It was an old literary reference.

Hyde grinned and stared at Dante like a large, graceless, hungry carnivore.

"Hi," Dante said. He approached the desk and pulled out a chair. Some men might have been intimidated by the mismatched pair of men, he supposed.

Dante could think of two things and two things only. The job ahead of him and the paycheck at the end of it.

CHAPTER TWO

The businessman inquired, "How was your trip, Mr. Shale?"

"Fine. No complications. Let's cut to the chase. What's the job? I'll warn you now, I don't do corporate espionage, and I expect straight dealings. Don't waste my time with euphemisms."

As he spoke, his emerald-hued, catlike eyes watched Slaine with an incredibly focused intensity. He examined the man, seeing him and seeing *through* him, his gaze leaving no place for deception or pretension to hide. It was the treatment he usually gave to first-time clients. It made an impression and emphasized the importance he placed on honesty.

Mr. Hyde noticed what was happening, leaned forward, and growled. Something *buzzed* like a mechanical echo through a rotary fan, but Dante ignored the man for the time being.

Slaine stared back in surprise. His right eye twitched around the lower lid. He sniffed, his nostrils flared, and he readjusted his posture within the broad and comfy expanse of his leather-backed chair. "I am unused to being spoken to in such a flippant manner, Mr. Shale," he stated in a low voice.

"Disrespectful," Hyde clarified, as though he assumed that Shale was too ignorant to know what *flippant* meant.

Dante turned his eyes toward the bodyguard. Not to give Slaine a break but simply to examine the massive bodyguard in more detail.

Everything about Hyde was paradoxical or seemed to clash with something else. It was as though someone had assembled him from spare parts. His skin was a deep bronze shade, but his eyes were a pale blue-grey, and his wild hair and bushy beard were reddish. The hair atop his head was a darker, rusty shade. The beard was more of a bright ginger orange. He had a broad jaw but a surprisingly narrow, almost fey nose.

His augmentations were the most attention-grabbing thing about him. He would've been a tall man to begin with. Cybernetics had given him added height, like someone wearing platform shoes, and straightened his spine, bringing him to just shy of seven feet tall. Metal and synthetics glimmered where skin should've been with occasional tubes visible under the skin—evidence of the hydraulics that had given him his original street name.

Back when he was a Reaper... Back when Dante had first heard about him and dismissed him as a thuggish monster, too bloodthirsty and psychopathic to ever be a true professional. It seemed that Mr. Slaine felt otherwise, though.

Dante ignored Hyde's implied threat and looked at the businessman.

"I was told you had a job for me. If you want to hire me, I need to hear about the job. That's all. You're not paying me for my company. The quicker we get on with it, the sooner you can get what you want—and the sooner I can get paid."

Slaine stared at him in amazement and said nothing.

Hyde clamped one of his hands on the back of Dante's chair, sending a vibration through it that shook the floor a little. "Oh, hell yes!" he guffawed. "I *like* this one. He's like the biggest little goldfish in a Londonburg pet shop, so confident that he'll eat fucking everyone when he gets to the ocean Dirtside. Maybe he could, though. That's the *fun* of it."

The natural tone of Hyde's voice had a harsh, snarling, bestial quality, like a guard dog making every sound it could think of to intimidate a trespasser. Due to his various augmentations, it also sounded processed. A synthetic crispness combined with a slightly echoing industrial undertone, as though someone had recorded a barking dog and forcibly edited the sound clips into a deranged parody of human speech.

Dante sat perfectly still. He didn't react either to Hyde's hand on the back of his chair or to the man's bizarre voice. No point in openly acknowledging such things. Still, inwardly he marveled at the fact that a creature like this could exist. Decades upon decades of technological advancement and transhumanist research, only to produce something that was, in essence, more robot than human.

"Yeah," Hyde added with a toothy leer. "I'm looking forward to working with him."

Dante blinked and looked at the monstrous bodyguard. "I'm confused. Are you the one offering me the job, or is he?" He glanced at Slaine, his eyes narrowing with mild annoyance.

Slaine snapped back from whatever had got into him. His shoulders twitched, his eyes closed and reopened, and he was once again the shrewd and confident businessman who stood astride the world.

"I am the one with the job. Any offer that you, or anyone else, receives here comes from me. The ideas are mine, the plans, and the strategies. I simply need people of sufficient quality to carry them out."

Watching him, Dante decided that Slaine was a pretty good actor. He hadn't recovered all of his cool. Part of him was still fazed and flustered. Still, he was doing an adequate job of hiding it and sliding back into his usual persona. Someone with less experience than Dante had at reading people might have fallen for the trick.

"Of course," Slaine added, "it would be ungracious of me to pretend that you aren't a remarkable man yourself, Mr. Shale. I've heard all about you. Everyone in Londonburg has, by now. See, Mr. Hyde?" He flourished his hand.

"This is the kind of quality we're paying for. Only the best. Dante Shale has faced down hordes of screaming Dirtwalkers while Earthside, all to bring a certain *objet d'art* back to its original owner. Those savages would certainly be unable to appreciate it themselves."

Dante nodded. The job to which Slaine referred was about two years ago, but he recalled it well. The Dirtwalkers, consumed with base survival and their primitive superstitions, had no inkling of the statuette's value. Since it was safe to say that it *didn't* give them magical protection, they were no worse off for having it snatched out from under their noses.

Slaine went on, "He's also faced the horrors of mutant Night-mutts and come back unscathed, making a pretty penny for our friendly competitors at Intra while he was at it. Little did Intra realize the magnitude of their mistake in turning him loose so I could hire him. No matter how mad, suicidal, or seemingly impossible a task, he always comes through. Skill, physical prowess, technical knowledge, and sheer bloody-minded willpower prevail. You're a rare specimen, Mr. Shale."

Dante flashed the man a smile. It faded quickly, though. Slaine had been smart enough to realize that he couldn't intimidate Dante, so he was now trying to flatter him instead.

"Thanks. Like I said, though, I'm here to talk business first and foremost."

A smirk of confidence was forming on the other man's face. It seemed that Slaine had another trick or two up his sleeve. "Business...and politics. As you might be aware, I am an alderman as well as an executive, so you might say that my ear is perpetually to the ground concerning any problems that might be swelling within our great society.

"The activities of Marauders such as yourself are increasingly a concern of the authorities. Many of them are worried that the upsets in fortune and finances created by your plundering expeditions are causing unnecessary instability. There is talk of enhanced regulation, higher taxes on the monies that change hands with clients, and so forth."

Dante frowned. He *wasn't* aware that the various bureaucrats and council members had been pontificating on such things. It didn't surprise him, but he'd been too busy lately to spend much time hanging out in pubs where people were liable to discuss politics.

"Yes," Slaine went on, his tone nearly wistful, "it's all growing far more complicated. The consequences of failure, noncompliance, and even the consequences of success are all greater than they used to be. It's one thing for a man to be fearless in the face of monsters in the wilderness.

"It takes another kind of courage to risk imprisonment, heavy fines, or the destruction of his reputation by the authorities. Not to say that such things are guaranteed to happen by any means. Let us say they're...within the realm of possibility, depending on what our government elects to do. Of course, no matter what the officials say, there is always a man's street reputation to consider. What the common folk think of him."

Dante's gaze was steady and even. Slaine's game was clearer now. He was trying to bait Dante into leaping at the job before hearing all about it by implying that he didn't have the guts to risk it. Or that he was afraid of looking like a fool and a coward to his legions of admirers among the average citizens.

Instead, he pushed all such concerns from his head and returned his focus to the original issue. "The job, Mr. Slaine. What exactly is it? Tell me that, and we can go from there. I have in fact turned down jobs before, because they were literally impossible according to everything I know. I've also succeeded at jobs that everyone else thought were *mostly* impossible. The difference is information. Whatever you know, tell me."

Slaine shook his head and blinked, drawing back as though someone had slapped him. "What?" he gasped in imitation shock. "You're saying that you doubt your abilities when it comes to difficult missions? That's not what I expected, least of all from you. I should think the *real* Dante Shale would promise to get the job done *no matter what*."

Dante snorted. He racked his brain for a second or two, trying to think of the most ridiculous thing possible. The first item that came to mind was his favorite celestial body.

"Mr. Slaine, if you had told me to fetch the moon and bring it back to your office, I couldn't because that's totally outside basic reality. I'm not going to make proclamations that I know can be proven false." He didn't blink. He only waited for the businessman's response.

While Hyde glowered at him with his unpleasant mixture of dislike and amusement, Slaine pretended to find Dante's comment amusing and let out a dry chuckle. "What would I want the moon for, Dante?"

"I don't know, and I don't care." He cracked his knuckles. "I don't claim to understand why the hell most people want most of the things they send me to retrieve. They usually don't tell me. It's rarely of any relevance anyway."

Mr. Hyde burst out laughing again, the metallic undertones sending a mild but unpleasant tremor through the roots of Dante's teeth.

"Oh, fucking yes, I love this *pendejo*. Can we keep him, *papi?*" Hyde turned his broad face toward his employer, his mouth contorted with what almost looked like hunger.

Slaine squirmed abruptly in discomfort, probably at the embarrassing nickname his servant had used. "Please give us a moment alone, Mr. Curtidor." It was an order rather than a request. His voice was low but icy.

Still laughing in his loud and unnatural voice, Hyde moved around from the side of the desk and clomped behind Dante's chair. "You better take the job, Shale. It's going to be way too much fun to miss. I promise! Ha, ha..." He rumbled off and disappeared into the antiseptic corridor.

Mr. Slaine leaned forward in his chair and folded his hands on the desk. He looked subtly irked that he'd failed to dominate the conversation. Still, he was sufficiently wily and thick-skinned that he was recovering quickly from Dante's abrasive demeanor and his bodyguard's obnoxious faux pas.

"All right, Shale, now that we're free of interruptions, I'll concede that you're right. Sometimes, it *is* best to get right down to business. Here is the nature of the job I have for you." Dante nodded and waited.

Slaine took a sphere out of his desk, pressed a few buttons, and watched as it hovered over the table, displaying a detailed three-dimensional map of the Earth's surface. It also holographically projected the outlines of the various elevated Stations encircling the Earth.

He pointed at Londonburg, floating above the island of Great Britain. "We're here, of course. You'll be going to America. Specifically, the Northeastern American Sunken Sprawl, here."

He pointed at a large island off the continent's eastern coast, not too far from Nova Scotia and Maine. "There you will encounter the remains of the suburbs and residential areas and outlying industrial zones that were once part of Atlantica Metro before it rose into the sky in 2138 C.E. There's an old research facility located there, and that's your target."

Dante looked at the globe. He'd never been to the original island, the place that had given its name by extension to the whole network of Stations now housing the bulk of civilized humanity. The tech advancements there—a combination of controlled development and "oh shit" events, according to historians—had led to this. But he had been all over the Earth, including to places most other Marauders and Plunderers refused to work.

"And?"

"I want a sample of an alloy from this facility. It was solely devoted to producing the substance, so you won't have any difficulty distinguishing it from other material that might have been lying around waiting to be processed. Time shouldn't have affected the samples' quality."

The Marauder scratched his chin, feeling the stubble grate against his fingertips. "How large does the sample have to be?"

"We need at least one kilogram of the alloy, a little over two pounds. We have reason to believe that there's substantially more than that in the facility, and if you can retrieve more, that would be better still. One kilogram is all that's required. Oh, and another thing..."

Dante arched his eyebrows.

"If possible, it would be best if you could recover the information on how to *produce* the alloy. Any research materials, academic papers, data storage devices, manuals, anything of that nature. No matter how old the technology or how obscure the language, I'm sure I can find the means to access and decipher it. However, I don't expect this. It would simply be a most wonderful bonus. The alloy itself is sufficient to complete your mission."

In a way, Dante was almost disappointed. What his new employer described so far was routine.

"Okay, Mr. Slaine. Jobs like this aren't unusual. I've run a lot of them. I'm perplexed why you were so adamant about getting *me* to do it. Why are you paying for the best of the best when a regular Marauder would do the trick as well? I passed a couple of them on the way up to your office. Souvanatong. Awir. They're good."

In referring to himself as the best of the best, Dante wasn't boasting but stating an objective fact. As for Ana and Ersan, it was also a fact that people didn't trifle with them. SSS could hire either of them far cheaper than they could hire Dante.

Unless...

Slaine smiled, and there was a suggestion of cruel mirth in it, as though part of him had been looking forward to this moment. "Ah. That leads us to the one major *wrinkle* in the job, you might say. A certain factor makes it far more dangerous than usual for a retrieval mission of this nature."

It figured. Dante wasn't shocked. He would've been more surprised if there *hadn't* been a nasty catch.

Slaine leaned back in his chair and steepled his fingers. "The research facility is overrun with Dirtwalkers, and not only the typical, run-of-the-mill savages with scrap metal spears and the like.

"This group has elevated itself to the status of something like an actual *kingdom* of the brutes. They're organized, surprisingly well-armed, and have shown that they're not afraid of Plunderers. Some carry stolen weapons and armor from Plunderers and Marauders whom they've caught and killed while trespassing on the planet."

Dante intuited the unspoken implications of this at once. Since he didn't like unspoken implications, he said them aloud. "You've tried this before. You hired other people, and they never made it back."

Once again, Slaine shifted uncomfortably in his seat. This time it seemed more like an affected gesture to lend gravitas to his request rather than a purely natural reaction to the unexpected.

"Correct." He sighed. "This tribe of Dirtwalkers—they call themselves the Harij—possess gear above and beyond what their kind would typically have, precisely because of a failed operation. I don't want to talk about that beyond what's directly relevant to your task—we'll provide you with all the information we gleaned from that operation, failure though it was."

Dante grunted. "Good. I haven't accepted yet. I'm glad you're thinking this through." Although Slaine was unctuous and over-ambitious, he at least didn't seem to be a moron. Dante had accepted jobs from clients who were astoundingly ignorant and irresponsible when it came to planning things out or providing useful intel to their hirelings.

Slaine gave a single slow nod. "Yes, of course. What I want from you, Dante Shale," he separated his hands and pointed at the Marauder's chest, "is the ironclad assurance that you can and will do the job if I can promise you a measure of tactical support."

"Such as?" Dante was curious. He was borderline impressed with Slaine's attention to strategy and conscious of how compli-cated such an operation could get. There was already more to it than simply dropping in, grabbing something, and running away.

Slaine gestured at the featureless corridor that led back to the security checkpoint. "Mr. Hyde will lead a team that will pose as Raiders and land somewhere near the facility. They'll kick up lots of dust, make a lot of noise, and so forth, thus drawing the bulk of the Harij force away for a while. Naturally, this will make it easier for you to slip into the facility and secure the true objec-tive. What do you say?"

It took about thirty seconds to weigh what Slaine had said against everything Dante knew and his past experiences with similar missions. "I say yes, Mr. Slaine. It's doable, provided you're telling me the whole truth. You've got yourself a deal."

The businessman's face split into an open grin for the first time. "Excellent! I'm so happy to hear that." He rose from his chair. Dante did likewise, and the two shook hands. Slaine's hand was soft. He'd likely never done dirty manual labor before. He had a surprisingly strong grip, though.

Slaine put a hand on Dante's shoulder, which was irritating, but there was no reason to suspect malevolent intent. They strolled across the penthouse den toward the hallway. The executive stated, "My people will be in touch, and we'll hash out the details shortly. The security detail will see you out. Oh, and don't mind Mr. Hyde—er, Curtidor—if you bump into him again. He lacks tact, but he's smart enough to understand how upset I would be if he did anything ill-advised."

With a chuckle, he turned and went back to his desk. Dante kept walking, reentering the antiseptic corridor, which felt like climbing into a pipe after the office's warm and airy vibe.

At the first juncture with a side hallway, an enormous black silhouette watched him pass and chortled, the sound close to a growl and buzzing with electric reverb. "Like I said, Shale. This is going to be *fun*."

CHAPTER THREE

No man was an island. When random people talked about Dante, they imagined him doing everything by himself. He was generally too busy to correct them, but occasionally he did when there was time and opportunity. His crew deserved that much if nothing else.

Going Dirtside was nothing to fuck around with. That was why Dante went with people he trusted.

"Hi, Dante."

He looked up. He'd been waiting near the corner, lounging against a bench with his face half-buried under the hood attached to his coat—that way, fewer people would recognize and pester him. As for Vivica Lamburg, he trusted her to identify him regardless.

He gave her a brief smile. "Hi, Viv." The many preparations they would have to make and the hardships they could look forward to overcoming occupied most of his thoughts, but it was nice to see his friends again.

Vivica was his quartermaster, responsible for gear and supplies. He relied on her to gather and organize things and cobble them together on the spot if needed. She was a slim woman of about his age, average height, freckled, with auburn hair and brown eyes. She wore a light jacket over tight but tasteful pants and a blouse. When on the job, she dressed less for casual fashion and more for pure comfort and convenience.

She came over and stood beside him to the left of the bench and had the decency to position herself to block him from the sight of most passersby. The crew knew about the problems of being a celebrity as well as Dante did.

He glanced at her. "Are you eating? No problems lately?"

She frowned, and her lips thinned. "Yes, I'm eating, and I'm fine. Why do you keep asking me? It's been over a year since *that* happened. I think we can acknowledge that it's in the past and leave it there. Please, and thank you."

He grimaced and exhaled. "Perhaps. I worry. I need you, besides. If something happens to you, I'll be out a major cog in our machine *and* a friend. I don't want either of those things to happen."

She bit her lip, trying not to blurt a response. Other pedestrians filed past them, paying them no heed, and vehicles both manned and automated zipped by on the thoroughfare or floated overhead in the sky lanes.

At length, she sighed. "Dante, I know what you mean, and I know you mean well. Sometimes your bluntness is almost a *disability*. If the ability to be polite and say things in ways that won't make people standoffish were a limb, you're missing one of yours."

He shrugged. "Sorry. I don't think I ever noticed it was missing, though. I seem to do fine with only four."

She laughed, but it was low and dry. "You're something else, Dante. So, when are Am and Des showing up? Are they going to meet us here, or can we go straight to the place and have them join us *there?*"

"Ambrose said he would meet us here. I'm not sure about Des. She said she would call you and let us know. The sooner, the better. We can't afford to stand on this corner all evening. Someone might think we're prostitutes."

Viv snorted. "You're not dressed for that job. Neither am I. Anyway, it's good to know that—oh, hold on, that might be her."

She reached into her pocket and pulled out her flattened sphere. Upon exposure to air, it immediately unfolded and expanded into its usual shape, rotating to the panel it generally used for phone calls.

Desiree's voice said, "Hi, I'm going to be late, so why don't I meet you at the place? What's it called, again?"

Dante leaned over Viv's shoulder and declared, "Rinaldo's." He also gave her the address, a nearby landmark, and the basic outline of directions, just to be safe.

"Oh, thanks. I'll be there. Sit tight. Bye." Des hung up, and the panel went dim.

Viv kept the sphere out a moment longer as she contemplated whether or not to call Ambrose. As she hit the button to disassemble the device back into a flat, pocketable mass, she and Dante spotted their third team member.

"Hullo," he called as he trudged toward them.

Ambrose Igento didn't seem like a shuttle pilot. The dark-skinned man with a mop of dark brown hair was thickset and morose, coming across as underconfident, but he was well aware of his impressive abilities. His ultra-casual attire fed into others' misconceptions about him.

Viv waved at him. "Hi, Ambrose. Des is going to be late, so we're heading straight to Rinaldo's. Good news, since I'm getting tired of waiting and want to eat." She looked sidelong at Dante. "See? I'm interested in eating. All is well."

"Noted." Dante clapped Am on the back. "Once you have time to come up with a flight plan, I'll want to look it over. In addition to getting to and from the Earth's surface, we'll also need you for tactical insertion and extraction, possibly on a leapfrogging basis depending on where the Dirtwalkers end up congregating."

Ambrose rubbed his nose. "You *always* want to look over the flight plan. When was the last time I let you down, Dante? Don't you have enough of your stuff to do that you can afford to trust me to take care of my job?"

All three were walking in the restaurant's direction, which was about a block and a half to the north. The buildings grew smaller but denser as they went. It was a pedestrian district, albeit mostly working-class.

Dante said, "It's mostly a formality, but it's important. I need a shuttle pilot of your skill, so I want to ensure you make it back every time along with the rest of us. You're not expendable."

Rinaldo's was one of those places where virtually anyone could eat and not feel too out of place. The vibe was casual but not slumming. The food was good and reasonably priced. The establishment attracted a different crowd depending on what time of day or day of the week it was.

The restaurant's street-facing front was almost entirely holographic, featuring a repetitive but tantalizing preview of the interior and some choice selections from its menu. Italian food was the main attraction, but they served a variety of other cuisine options, including a few generally regarded as unique to present-day Londonburg.

It was busy, too, with a crowd bustling outside the door. Dante pushed past them, grateful that his hood was still keeping him anonymous. Vivica and Ambrose were close on his heels.

An automated hosting service placed them at a table off in the east wing. Fortunately, they weren't rubbing shoulders too closely with the other guests. They barely had time to examine the drink menus when a familiar figure hurried in and looked around before settling eyes on them.

"Oh, there's Des," Viv piped up. "I thought it would take her longer." She waved, and the final member of the crew ambled up.

Desiree Naphtalim was a curvy young woman with a dusky complexion and a green streak in her hair, which oddly complemented her deep almond eyes. She was the crew's communications expert, sending messages between everyone else, notably to and from Dante when he was out on the surface. She also handled all sorts of scanners and cameras, drawing the appropriate conclusions as necessary.

She put her hair in order as she approached their table. "Sorry I'm late. I had a slight mishap or two in getting the hell out of my room. Credit issues. I was a little too absorbed in reading up on things in advance. Political stuff, mostly."

Ambrose pushed out a chair for her. "You're only 'late' in the loosest sense of the term. We haven't ordered drinks yet."

A young man with a polite but somber demeanor approached, wearing an apron. "Well, now's your chance," he quipped, having overhead the end of the exchange. "My name's Erik, and I'll be your waiter. Do you know what you want to drink yet?"

Dante and Viv ordered kombucha beer. Desiree requested a particularly decadent fruity cocktail. Am didn't drink alcohol and ordered regular kombucha instead. Dante also did what he usually did when they ate out—he ordered food on everyone else's behalf by mixing and matching a variety of stuff they all liked and placing it on a single tab. The others rarely had cause to complain.

"Sounds good," Erik muttered while checking the entries on his sphere after it finished recording what they'd said. "I'll get those back to you right away." He hurried off.

Once he departed, Dante wasted no time turning to his partners and getting straight to the meat of the coming discussion. He flexed and unflexed his hands. His jaw set as he stared across the table with a steady, even expression of low-grade intensity.

"Okay. I gave you the extremely short version before, so you all have an idea of the job. Here's the long version, followed by my plans for the best way to go about it."

None of them made sarcastic comments or asked unnecessary questions. All simply leaned forward, listening intently and watching as the Marauder spoke. It was rare for them to have major disagreements with Dante's schemes anyway, but he always gave them the chance to disagree or contribute their opinions before he decided on a course of action.

"We're going Dirtside, obviously," he began. "The old island of Atlantica, the Northeastern Sprawl around where the city used to be. There's a facility there—the client is getting me the coordinates as we speak—which I need to infiltrate to gain a one kilogram sample of some alloy. They also want me to get plans for how to produce the alloy if possible, but it's not required."

He wasn't too surprised when his friends asked essentially the same questions he had in Slaine's office. What was so strange and noteworthy about that? Why did they need an outfit as elite and expensive as Dante's to carry it out?

He smiled grimly. "There's a catch."

Ambrose pinched the bridge of his nose. "There's *always* a catch when it sounds too good to be true. Let me guess, Night-mutts everywhere? Dangerously high radiation levels?"

"Worse," Dante said. "An unusually smart, well-equipped, and well-organized tribe of Dirtwalkers called the Harij controls the whole place. I've never heard of them, but if they have an actual name that high-end clients are aware of, they must be a pretty fucking big deal. They took out another team of Plunderers the client sent previously and looted their armor and weapons. Bad stuff. The good news is that our new employers will help provide a nice diversion."

He then outlined the general nature of Slaine's plan. It sounded good on paper, but now that more time had passed since his meeting with the executive, Dante turned over more and more possibilities for how it could all go wrong.

Still, if he couldn't think of solutions to those potential problems, he was pretty damn sure his crew could. They'd always come through before.

"Hmm." Desiree pondered it, her dark eyes distant with deep

thought. "It sounds perfect, which means that in real life, there'll probably end up being some God-awful thing we never could've thought of that'll pop up at the last second and ruin everything. Then again, you've always been good at getting your ass out of those situations, Dante."

Viv tittered. "Too true. Planning makes a lot of difference, but being able to improvise can make *the* difference."

Ambrose seemed distracted. "What I want to know, and I'm sure everyone else wonders as well…who exactly is this mysterious 'high-end client' of whom you speak, Dante?"

Without hesitating or missing a beat, he told them. "Cormac Slaine. And by extension, SSS."

A heavy silence fell over the table. It looked as though all three of them wanted to blurt further questions or comments, but their waiter was returning with their drinks, so they all shut up for the time being. It was better not to discuss jobs in too much detail with third-party individuals hanging around nearby. Especially in the current politically charged social climate that increasingly pervaded the whole city.

The waiter announced, "Hey there, back with the beverages. It'll be a few minutes on the food yet. Enjoy and let me know if you need anything else."

"Sure," Dante said. "Thanks."

Everyone grabbed their respective drink and took a long, leisurely swig. By the time they did, the waiter was long gone.

Des glanced from side to side. "SSS is about as high-end as it gets. That would explain why they're paying so well. It also makes me nervous. I won't lie. Slaine might be a big important rich guy and all, but his reputation...not so good, when you dig into it."

Dante didn't doubt that she had *already* dug into it. Desiree had a habit of researching things in her spare time, even when they weren't immediately pertinent to work or survival.

"Yeah," Am echoed. "Like employing that Hyde guy, I forget his original name. We heard about him before. The dude is a monster and ought to be in prison somewhere. Or better yet, jettisoned into space with a one-way ticket and no life suit. Pretty sure Slaine pulled some strings to be able to employ the bastard and keep the authorities at bay."

Des nodded curtly in the pilot's direction before resuming with, "That too. I was mainly thinking of all the shady business dealings Slaine's gotten involved with. Some of that crap is pretty much an open secret by now. He's lucky his company's value is so astronomical, and of course, they're vital enough to the economy here that the local authorities keep turning a blind eye to it all."

Vivica added, "A lot of the local authorities are probably in on it themselves. It's cheaper to bribe a politician than comply with a regulation. Or to hire a team of lawyers to fend off an investigation. It's not only Londonburg. All the Atlantica Stations are starting to use SSS's solar collection tech."

He listened to their concerns and understood them, but on some level, Dante simply didn't care that much. Such things weren't for him to decide or deal with. He wasn't a bureaucrat, corporate executive, or an elected official. He was simply a professional.

His sharp swipe made it clear to his people that he considered such discussions pointless.

"Never mind all of that," he snapped. "It's not part of our job to assess every aspect of what our clients do in their spare time or judge them on a moral basis. The only things we need to do are assess *the job itself* and judge whether or not they're likely to pay. If Slaine is comfortable handing out bribes, he can pay us for our work, however slimy he might be."

Then something else occurred to Dante, and he smiled with a certain vicious, sardonic satisfaction. "Besides, I'm famous. If he tries to cheat me—us—it will impact his popularity in a big way. He's a pompous, wily bastard, as near as I can tell, but the impression he made on me is that he's taking this operation seriously and will do everything the smart way, by the book."

His crew members looked back at him without speaking. Each of them had doubts in their minds, and he could all but read their exact thoughts on their faces. Expansions of what they had said aloud, for one. Dim fears that they might be getting in over their heads—that at last, they'd taken on the job that would prove too much even for their substantial abilities and leave them not rich and happy but silent and rotting in the dust of a broken world.

They'd had similar doubts before. Every time, they'd somehow pulled through. The one person who was always in the thickest of the shit, who bore the most risk and the most responsibility, was Dante himself. That made a difference.

Viv sighed. "Fine, I guess. Since this will be an especially stressful and high-intensity job, from the sound of it, could you do me one favor, Dante? Could you please *not* do that thing where you keep compulsively checking on my health and second-guessing my loadout of your gear? It would make life easier."

Her tone implied that she wasn't *that* upset. He supposed it was still a legitimate complaint.

"Yeah," Ambrose added, "or, for that matter, that thing where you critique my flight plans by pointing out all the ways we could get killed if I pull it wrong or come in too fast? Seeing as how I *never* do that. I mean, come on, man."

Dante laughed, but before he could respond, Desiree interrupted. She wasn't about to be left out.

"Or, that thing where you ignore my warnings and argue with the readings I'm giving you, despite their base in technology that can see and hear farther than you can?" She swirled her fingertip around the rim of her glass. "Just a thought."

Dante rubbed his eyes. "Yeah, okay, I'll do my best. You guys always do yours. I like to be confident that we're all doing the damn thing right. It's served us well all these years, hasn't it?"

"True," Viv conceded, "but how does that old saying go? It's not the years. It's the mileage."

Their waiter reappeared, bringing their food on a broad hovering tray. Am's head snapped toward it. "Ah, a distraction," he observed. "Probably just what we needed."

Dante interjected, "Before you get your mouths full, are we taking this job or not? I am. If you don't want to, I'll find someone else. I'd rather have you three."

They all looked at him with narrowed, skeptical eyes.

"Of course," Des retorted. "You'd get killed without us, and all of your fans would be mad at *us* about it."

CHAPTER FOUR

"Oh, my…" Desiree remarked, ogling the monstrosity that lay before them. "That thing is ugly. I guess when size and volume are the only stuff you prioritize, you end up with abominations like that."

SSS owned but didn't publicly advertise the small starport they'd come to. On the trip there, Dante deduced that Slaine's people had cleared most of the civilian traffic away to offer them further privacy. After all, what Mr. Hyde and his crew would be doing was officially off the books.

Once past the usual gauntlet of walls, fences, electrobarriers, and security checkpoints, the trio stood on the balcony that over-looked the loading bay before the gates that led out of the gravitic sphere and into space itself. Dante, Viv, and Des were all there.

Ambrose had gone separately to fly their shuttle into the port from the public one he'd had it at previously. It lay there in the far corner, unobtrusive but sleek. Dante had always thought it a handsome vessel. It wasn't flashy and didn't indicate fabulous wealth or cutting-edge bells and whistles, but it did give the impression of being exactly what it was. A well-made, well-maintained vehicle piloted by dedicated pros who had nothing to prove.

As for the Reaper vessel Hyde and his people would take, the impression it gave was more analogous to something that had no single rhyme or reason behind its design. It could pull off the required job anyway by disregarding aesthetics and taste. It was a bloated, rambling, ungainly ship, dark and haphazard, but it looked mechanically sound. The craft was more than sufficient to hold enough men to keep the Dirtwalkers busy and create the appearance of a real and purposeful plunder raid.

Speaking of which, Dante could tell at a glance that Hyde's crew were mostly the real deal. Actual Reapers, in many cases, and in others, mercenaries who might well have done Reaper work on the side when more respectable gigs weren't available. It seemed fitting, given who their boss would be.

Hyde himself was nowhere in sight yet. The men and women he was bringing with him were loading up supplies, doing safety inspections, or simply lounging around chatting and smoking.

Ambrose was still in the cockpit of his shuttle. He wasn't the sociable type, so Dante didn't blame him for not wanting to get out and mingle with the roughnecks and cutthroats. In any event, his friends had now arrived.

Vivica eyed their new partners. "Well, they look like men who probably have experience killing Dirtwalkers," she observed in a dry, flat tone. "That much, at least, is good to know."

"Yeah," Dante grunted. "As long as they can pull off their end of the mission, that's all I care about. It's the only thing that needs to concern any of us. We'll have plenty of issues of our own to focus on. Let's get down there and keep Ambrose company. He looks lonely."

Des chuckled. "He usually does. Anytime he's somewhere in civilization and has to deal with people. Space suits him better than the Stations do, I think."

"Probably." Dante was well aware of his friends' capabilities and limitations. For the moment, his main concern was ensuring they had all the appropriate gear. Plus the unpleasant but necessary task of finding where Eduardo H. Curtidor was hiding and conferring with him on schedule and protocol. The two crews would have to coordinate their insertions with a *very* high degree of synchronization.

The three walked down the balcony and toward the ramp, descending to the bay. Theirs and Hyde's were the only ships present, barring a service vehicle native to the port itself that sat forgotten in the far corner. Hyde's people and their vessel took up two-thirds of the available space. The Reaper ship was, after all, intended to transport large quantities of booty from Earth to the Stations. It *had* to be big.

It looked as though some of the mercs had noticed Dante's arrival but more or less willfully ignored him until he, Viv, and Des were within conversational distance. Now one of them turned, rubbed his hands, and approached them.

"So," he began, in a slightly nasal voice, "you're Shale and friends, am I right?" He was pale and wiry, not imposing, but there was enough scrappy toughness that Dante wouldn't have written him off as a serious opponent.

Dante inclined his head. "Yes. Our pilot brought our gear, and I understand Mr. Slaine has made a few other things available for us, which you guys would handle. We'll need those, and we'll also need to review our timetables before we depart. Is Hyde around?"

The pale man chuckled. "Well, it's true then, isn't it? No wasting time on bullshit formalities. Nice crew, also." He shot sly glances at Viv and Des. "Yeah, Mr. Hyde is onboard. I'll get him in a second. Why don't you guys do inventory or something in the meantime?"

Desiree muttered in obvious discomfort, "Yes, that sounds

like an *excellent* idea. I'll go talk to Ambrose." She turned and strode toward their ship.

Viv lingered, holding Dante's gaze. "I already did inventory, but you always want to double-check it. Want to get it out of the way now?"

Dante considered it for a second. "No. See if Des and Am need help with anything. I'm going to wait here in case Hyde shows up. That way we can get this all wrapped up as quickly as possible."

"Suit yourself," Viv replied. "Be careful." She put a slim hand on Dante's arm, then turned and followed Desiree to the shuttle.

Dante turned and watched the Reaper ship and its crew. He had a good measure of the vehicle and the men by now and decided that his initial impression had been correct. Dangerous people, all of them, but probably competent.

What still perplexed him was Slaine's role in their presence. He wondered if the clean-cut executive had a personal hand in procuring such a crew or if he'd simply given Hyde carte blanche to gather whatever band of pirates and thugs he wanted. The exact nature of Slaine's and Hyde's working relationship and how it intersected with the "official" business of SSS was still mysterious to him.

It didn't matter, though, provided everything went *mostly* according to plan.

His brief reverie was interrupted by a distinctively synthetic, echoing voice—loud, rough, and bellowing—that rattled out of the huge ship and instantly caught the attention of everyone who could hear it. The various pirates and mercs stopped what they were doing, tensed, or turned their heads toward the ramp that led to the big shuttle's passenger door.

The first few words were unintelligible, but at the end, Dante caught, "...about fucking time. This is getting boring! Why didn't someone tell me they were here?"

Dante waited motionlessly and stared at the ramp. The Reapers returned to whatever they were doing as Mr. Hyde clanked out the door and descended to the loading bay's floor.

"Hey!" he announced when he saw Dante, and a broad, toothy grin split his face amid his red beard. "I thought you were going to be late. That doesn't suit your reputation, does it, Shale? Ha, ha. Of course, we're giving you all the easy, boring shit to do. We'll be the ones pounding Dirtwalkers into a fine paste." He thumped his armored chest with a hydraulically-augmented fist. The sound was like a heavy lid falling over a ventilation shaft.

Dante made a show of glancing at a holographic clock in the corner. "We were four minutes early." He looked back at Hyde. "It won't take us more than ten minutes to be ready to go, as far as our gear and everything else goes. We need to go over the plan again and ensure everyone coordinates this right."

Hyde snorted and laughed, but the pale man drawing closer to the conversation gave a begrudging nod. "Yeah, good idea," he drawled. "Mr. Slaine will be here soon to help with that, won't he, Mr. Hyde?"

Hyde abruptly looked at the smaller man. "You weren't supposed to tell," he growled. The low frequencies of his voice raised the hackles on the back of Dante's neck despite himself. The pale guy squirmed in place but managed not to flinch.

Dante pointed out, "It doesn't matter. If he's coming here anyway, I'll wait to discuss things when he arrives. Give me ten minutes to check things over with my crew."

He turned and strode toward the smaller shuttle before the Reapers could protest, although Hyde made a few halfhearted snarling and grumbling sounds at his back.

When Dante climbed through the ship's opened hatch,

Ambrose was the first to greet him from where he sat in the cockpit, double-checking the vehicle's controls. "Hi, Dante. That was fast. Maybe we lucked out and won't have to spend too much actual time interacting with those...people."

Dante settled into the copilot's seat and shook his head. "No such luck. Slaine is coming to inspect things personally, and we'll be reviewing the plans then. Until he gets here, I figured we'd do our final inspection routine. Show me the flight plans again."

Sighing, Am pulled out his sphere and brought up the plans. Both he and Dante had looked at them previously, but the Marauder insisted on triple-checking them no matter what. For a mission of this level of complexity, even Am probably agreed it was a good idea.

His slight frown and obvious discomfort likely had more to do with the unpleasant prospect of having to speak to Hyde and his men, Dante guessed. Or Slaine, for that matter.

The flight plans weren't too complicated aside from the ending portion when they would need to pinpoint the alloy facility. Dante found them satisfactory after only about two or three minutes of review. Then he went over to the far corner of the cockpit area, where Desiree sat in silence beside the viewing and comms equipment.

"Everything is in good working order," she reassured him. "See for yourself."

He nodded and inspected it. The radios, cameras, and sensors were all in equally good shape as they'd been before Am had dropped him off at the port the other day.

Patting Des on the shoulder, he stood again. "Excellent. I'm going to talk to Viv. Assuming Mr. Slaine arrives on time, we'll all need to head out to finish our little discussion after that. Don't worry. The job is the important thing. It doesn't matter what stupid comments anyone makes."

He said it loud enough that Am and Des could hear it. Neither reacted in an obvious way, but there was a faintly perceptible shift in their posture and demeanor that told him they'd heard. He wondered if they were surprised that he'd shown concern, if only briefly, for their feelings.

Vivica was going over their supplies in the back, as she should be. "I overheard," she said. "Not looking forward to it, but it will be over in a few minutes. Then it's all chasing the paycheck, right? Anyway, go ahead and check. I'm pretty sure you'll be satisfied."

Dante almost smiled. "Probably." He took the inventory list from her and did a quick visual scan of their stores, confirming that everything they needed was present and in the correct place.

Emergency supplies to keep them alive if by some horrible chance they crashed. Medical stuff. Tools and fuel for the ship itself. And weapons, of course. The Atlantica Stations didn't permit the use of projectile armaments or explosives since the risk of damaging and disrupting the gravitech implements surrounding the cities was too great.

Anyone who needed to do violence made do with hand-to-hand weaponry. The naked fist was still a viable choice for those who knew how to use it. Otherwise, people defended themselves with everything from crude knives and pipes to highly advanced razorfists and electric batons.

Dirtside, it was another story altogether. There were no rules to speak of down there, and the only collateral damage would be to the hostile half-mutants, to creatures even worse than Dirt-walkers, or to the blasted and desolate landscape itself. The crew had a fairly impressive arsenal of traditional projectile weapons, pulsecore carbines, military-grade plasma cutters, and a box of grenades, along with a couple of dart guns and crossbows for stealth work.

Dante intended to take a razorfist, a pulsecore, and a couple of grenades. Barring some massive catastrophe, there was no reason to suspect he would need more than that. The heavy weaponry was mostly for the rest of the crew in case things degenerated into an open battle.

He finished checking the inventory, nodded his approval, and led Viv into the cockpit area. "All right, let's head out. Slaine might have some final tidbit of info for us as well. I hope he's on time."

Begrudgingly, they all got to their feet. Dante led them through the hatch, where they stood on an open floor section in front of their shuttle. They positioned themselves in plain sight for anyone looking for them, but not at the forefront or otherwise obtrusive. That was the way Dante liked it. Being showy led to problems.

Off to the left, Hyde and his men laughed and joked around between doing the last of their checkups. A couple of guys looked over and saw Ambrose, stared at him, and nudged one another.

"Hey," one called. "I think they sent you the wrong pilot. Shouldn't that guy be programming games or something?" His buddy snickered.

Ambrose's jaw tightened, but he otherwise didn't react.

Dante didn't feel like coming up with a clever comeback. He glared, mentally disemboweling the man.

Before peace could settle in, machinery whirred, and Hyde clomped between them. "Hey! Are you guys harassing my men?"

Viv glared at the monstrous Reaper. "No. Other way around."

"Oh? Really?" Hyde turned to the two guys, his face distorting in a grin. "How dare you hurt the feelings of those poor kids. I mean, look at them. They're probably too fragile for this work, and Shale is taking them out to break them in. Be more considerate!"

There was no subtlety to his sarcasm, but half of the mercs found it funny regardless. Or at least, they pretended to chuckle. It might have been purely an act of diplomacy to stay on their commander's good side.

Dante maintained his blank, neutral expression. He'd encountered nonsense like this many times. Hyde was trying to get a reaction out of them as an excuse to escalate things to a shouting match, or better yet an actual fight. That his boss was paying him to work *with* Dante's crew had been forgotten next to his primitive need for pointless conflict.

Then sounds wafted down from the checkpoint beyond the balcony, the noise of a significant crowd of people moving at a brisk pace. Dante glanced up. A platoon of fully decked-out security officers tramped onto the overhang with Cormac Slaine carefully sequestered in their midst. His bodyguards knew how to move and handle their weapons and checked everything around them for threats, but the whole spectacle looked less like a sensible security operation than a military parade intended as a show of force.

They descended the ramp, with the frontmost ranks spreading out to go through the motions of securing the area before the central ring of men came down and discharged Slaine himself onto the bay. The rear echelon remained on the ramp. Both Dante's and Hyde's crew watched with faint curiosity and half-bored amusement.

Slaine advanced to the open space between the two crews and adjusted his tie. In his element and surrounded by his entourage, Dante had to admit that the businessman did a pretty good job commanding the space around him and projecting a vibe of suave importance.

"Good morning," he began, speaking vaguely to the entire workforce, although he looked back and forth between the two crews every few seconds. "I would like to spend a moment reviewing the plans before turning you all loose. I have the utmost confidence in you. Provided, of course, that you do exactly as instructed."

At that last bit, he looked pointedly at Hyde, and his gaze lingered for a second too long for it to be a coincidence. Hyde smirked.

Slaine went on. "Roughly, the operation will involve Mr. Curtidor's team launching first, setting down in the wastes outside the former Atlantica Sprawl, and picking a fight with the local hostiles. Mr. Shale's team will hover or circle as needed to give Team A the time they need to draw off most of the opposition. Then they'll land at the specified coordinates and infiltrate the facility. Once Shale has the payload, Team B will contact Team A and have them break off the attack, at which point both teams will return directly to Londonburg Station."

Dante said, "Correct."

Slaine eyed him briefly, probably annoyed once more at his direct way of speaking and lack of deference, but he smiled. "I am glad you have such a firm handle on things, Mr. Shale."

Then the executive turned back to Hyde. "Remember, stick to *only* doing what—"

"Yeah, yeah," Hyde growled, leering with mirth. "I heard you the first time. Hell, the man thinks my hearing is going. Hah! I had that augmented along with everything else. I can hear the way people's underpants swish."

Slaine glared while the men tried not to laugh, uncertain whether it was riskier to incur the wrath of the hulking Reaper or his master. Any reaction could potentially antagonize one or both.

Slaine turned his gaze lazily away from Hyde, and when he spoke next, he again addressed the entire chamber. "Mr. Curtidor thinks it's funny to speak this way as a game. I only tolerate him because he can do the jobs I hired him for. I expect the same of all of you."

Dante nodded. "We'll get it done. You'll get your sample, Mr. Slaine. Count on it."

The businessman adjusted his tie once more and smoothed his hair. "Good. I trust you've gone through your preparations as far as the specifics are concerned. Good luck, gentlemen and ladies. I have a lunch to go to, so I'll take my leave."

He turned on one heel and marched up the ramp, his elite guard moving in tandem and the vanguard waiting to bring up what was now the rear.

Once they were out of sight, Dante looked at Mr. Hyde, who was muttering something to one of his troops in a low voice that sounded like static feedback. "Four minutes' head start is enough for you guys?"

Hyde waved a hydraulic paw. "Yeah, plenty. We'll heat things up for you, heh, heh. You'll get to do the easy part. Breaking in your, uh, *crew* will be nice and easy."

Desiree snorted. "They should try doing our job sometime. See how—"

Dante put a hand firmly on her shoulder. "Save it. Let's get back to the shuttle. Watch them and time it so we're perfectly within the scheduled timeframe. Ambrose, you can always speed us up or slow down to keep the four-minute window."

"Got it," the pilot acknowledged. "Then they'll see how well I can fly."

They returned to the ship, an odd feeling of determination and camaraderie growing between them. It was rare for the quartet to work with anyone else, and the prospect of being treated like second-stringers by Hyde's motley band made them all the more eager to prove that they had *earned* their reputation.

As usual, Dante would sit up front to observe and function as the closest thing the shuttle had to a copilot. Ambrose would handle the bulk of the flying. Vivica and Desiree sat in the two seats farther back, making it easier to access the communications equipment in Des' case or the rear storage area in Viv's.

The seats were comfortable enough. Although not state-of-the-art, they were nonetheless modern and of good quality. They functioned as perfectly normal chairs under relaxed conditions but had the necessary accouterments for handling a powerful launch from a gravity well.

In this instance, they only had to get outside Londonburg's

field, which extended far enough past the station to bind in external space traffic going around the periphery of the city-state. Once they broke free of it, pointed toward Earth, the planet's gravity would seize them and bring them in.

The real difficulty was making sure they descended at precisely the right spot. The Northeastern American Sunken Sprawl was a good distance west across the Atlantic from the site of Old London, which lay more or less directly beneath Londonburg.

It would help that the Reapers were going down first. In theory, Am could follow them most of the way and divert at the end after they made their landing and began their diversionary operation. Still, hitting the alloy facility would require immense precision.

Dante asked, "You got all your coordinates, Am? Route planned out?"

"Of course." A faint hint of exasperation came through in his voice. "Whenever do I not?"

Dante let out a low chuckle. "True. Whenever do I not *ask?* I have faith in you. Do your thing."

Des quipped, "That's odd, Dante. You're friendlier than usual. Even you must be a little bit anxious about this job..."

He grimaced, deciding to say nothing. It would be better for Ambrose to focus on his job rather than worrying about how anyone did or didn't feel.

They heard the Reapers' ship powering up while the barriers lowered over the bay, safeguarding the rest of Londonburg Station from the soon-to-be-opened hatch. The noise was impossible to miss or ignore. Am began powering everything up so they'd be ready to blast off after the bigger shuttle departed. While he handled that, Dante did the minor task of adjusting the cabin pressure regimen to account for the stresses of jumping from one gravitational field to another.

"Here goes," Desiree murmured. She watched on one of the

monitors as Hyde's ship ground forward, the thrusters turning on as it cleared the station's edge and slipped out into the void of space.

Dante pointed at Ambrose.

The smaller shuttle roared to full life as they all felt the familiar sensation of the ship lurching forward, out the opened hatch, and into the blackness beyond. Londonburg's gravity tried to cling to them, but they broke free of it, and lightheadedness set in as they entered the short span of relatively "free" space between the pull of the two bodies. Their gravity device hummed to counteract the beginnings of weightlessness.

Ahead of them, Earth loomed.

Then, seemingly only a minute later, the turbulence began as the shuttle's nose pierced the exosphere, with the increased resistance of the thermosphere ahead.

Any moment now, the friction of penetrating through the planet's atmosphere would create flames and other interference that blotted out the front view, and they would need to rely on other methods of navigation until things cleared out. For the moment, Earth loomed closer as the blackness of space receded to the sides. The sheer size of the planet, compared to any one of the Atlantica Stations—even Londonburg, which was one of the biggest—was always breathtaking.

Earth had once been primarily blue and green, wrapped in wispy white clouds. These days it was a motley amalgamation of colors, but they all seemed somehow duller than anything Dante had seen in the old photos and videos. The oceans were a dark slate color rather than vibrant blue, and the land was mostly dead brown. The clouds alternated between white, grey, and yellow, with occasional flashes of red and green.

Then the flames burst forth. It was a normal part of atmospheric reentry, and the ship's hull materials could easily repel the heat and remain unscathed. Still, Dante recalled that for people new to space travel, it was usually one of the most unnerving parts of the process.

When the fiery shower was over, they hovered directly above the former home of their species in all its wrecked and ruined glory.

CHAPTER FIVE

Ambrose pointed. "There it is. Old Atlantica Metro, or what's left of it. Never seen the place before myself. You know, it looks better than I would've guessed for being as old as it is."

Dante nodded, watching the derelict and long-devastated city grow larger in their field of view as the clouds thinned and they drew closer. It was a fascinating, almost awe-inspiring sight. Still, his chief interest was in evaluating its layout, weak points, areas of maximum danger, and the best avenues to make his entrance and exit.

Plus the facility itself. That was the most important thing.

Desiree spoke up. "The coordinates Slaine gave us aren't as precise as we hoped. They'll get us within about a mile, maybe half a mile if we're lucky, but we'll have to scout for the place based on visual feedback and the descriptions we have from the failed previous missions."

"Roger," said Ambrose. "We'll be right within the square they specified in about one minute. I don't see the Reaper ship. Have they made landfall yet?"

Dante paid close attention to what both of them said.

"Yes," Des confirmed. "They're off starboard and behind us.

They're touching down right now. So far I don't see any Dirt-walker activity, but if the intel was accurate and the, um, whatever this tribe is called are based here, they ought to be swarming out directly."

Viv said, "The Harij. That's their name."

"Yeah," Dante muttered. "Am, circle until we see some activity from the locals. If we have to delay longer than four minutes, we will. Des, radio the Reapers and ask them for an update. They might've seen or scanned something that we haven't."

The sky had been largely clear when they had first come in, but now a mass of clouds rolled over the horizon toward them on a powerful wind, bringing with it dust and thunder. The clouds were a disturbing mottle of dark orange and dull green, probably due to a reaction between the chemical compounds released into the atmosphere since the planet had lost the battle against pollution.

Ambrose had noticed. "I can do that for a few extra minutes, but once that storm comes in, I'll have to land *somewhere*. That green shit always wreaks havoc on our sensors and puts extra strain on the atmospheric filter."

"I know," Dante grunted. "Do what you can. Des, contact Hyde's men."

Sucking in her breath, Des paged them and got a response almost instantly.

"Hello, yes? Team B? We have made landfall. Troops are ready for deployment. Dirtwalkers are watching us nearby. They *think* they're hidden. Ha, ha. Probably they're scared to attack the ship. We'll send men out, so they try to ambush us. Then the reserves will join the attack. Over."

Desiree said, "That sounds good, but don't waste time. There's a storm rolling in, and we need to land ASAP. Over."

Abruptly there came the sounds of grunting and shuffling and a metallic *clanking*. Then a more familiar voice came through, sending an unpleasant vibration through the shuttle's sound system.

"We're not wasting any fucking time," Hyde snarled. "*They* are. We're taking the fight to them right now. You boys and girls just watch. Have a good time now. Out."

The radio went silent.

Vivica remarked, "For once, I appreciate his enthusiasm." She pointed at the screen. "I'd be surprised if that big square building there *isn't* our place. It sure looks like an industrial facility to me. More of a complex of buildings, but they seem to be all connected by covered hallways or something. Maybe to keep moisture from contaminating the alloy? Atlantica used to get a lot of rain."

Dante squared his jaw. "I think you're right. It's within our coordinates. As soon as we see the Reapers moving out to engage, take us down to that empty lot behind the wall there, about a block from the facility."

"Okay," said Am. "That's close enough that if any of them are still nearby, they'll notice us easily."

Dante's grin would've been frightening to anyone who didn't already know and trust him. "Leave that to me." He tightened the razorfist on his left wrist and flexed his fingers and hand muscles.

Less than a minute later, Des reported that half of the Reapers' force was marching out of their ship. Enough to catch the attention of the Harij and hopefully inspire them to send all available warriors out. Then the other half would circle and trap the Dirtwalkers in the middle. It was an old tactic from ancient history lessons.

In the back of his mind, Dante wondered what the casualty rates for both forces would be. The Harij probably outnumbered them by a substantial factor, but then again they lacked the training or equipment to be anywhere near as effective on a one-to-one basis. Still, according to Slaine, they were a cut above the usual mouth-foamers and had captured modern weapons. The Reapers might well lose at least a few of their men.

There was also the possibility that Hyde would think it was funny to annihilate every last one of the Harij. The Atlantica Stations tried to rein in *excessive* violence against Dirtwalkers but rarely enforced such measures. The primitive and barbaric peoples of Earth had no legal standing in the Stations.

Ambrose sailed toward the spot Dante had indicated, slowing to a hover as he tried to come in without being too obvious. In a way, the growing wind from the coming storm was a good thing since it howled through the ruins loudly enough that their shuttle's noise was less obtrusive.

They also had a cloaking device that helped somewhat. Like most such tech, it was calibrated mainly for use in space or around the Stations and didn't work as well on Earth. It might obscure the ship enough to elude casual notice, but anyone looking carefully at their location would be able to tell what was going on.

As their pilot did his work, Dante got up and checked himself over, ensuring he had everything he needed. His weapons, his sphere, his collapsible first-aid kit, his radio, and the case. It would easily hold a kilogram of the alloy, possibly more, and have room for papers, data storage devices, or other mechanisms the facility's staff might've used to store information.

He closed his eyes, inhaled through his nose, and breathed out through his mouth.

"I'm ready," he proclaimed. "Put us down. Des, what's up with our friends?"

She glanced at him before returning her gaze to the screens. "They're moving toward—whoa! All hell just broke loose. I'd estimate at least fifty Dirtwalkers coming from the ruins, frontal attack, and about the same number moving in on their flanks from the hills. Some of them have guns and helmets." In a low, skeptical tone, she added, "Hope that Hyde guy knows what he's doing."

Viv squeezed Dante's hand. "They know what they signed up for and are equipped to handle it. Focus on your safety and getting the job done. Okay?"

He looked at her eyes, showing her a flash of warmth before he refocused on the task at hand. "Okay. But there isn't really a *safe* way to do this. Only a *right* way."

The shuttle touched down near the lot's cracked concrete surface. A high yet broken wall with steel girders and pipes sticking out of it like bleached bones shielded them from the nearby facility. There were no obvious Harij sentries nearby.

Before departing, Dante popped out his little oxygen inhaler and took two puffs. He only used it when he expected to be Dirtside for an hour or more. Although not deadly, Earth's atmosphere could cause a slow deterioration in respiration, particularly for people who spent most of their time in the Stations. The Dirtwalkers had adapted to it. Dante had prowled around the planet enough that he probably handled it better than the average Atlantican, but he preferred not to take needless risks.

"Okay," he said. "Back shortly. Radio silence unless it's especially dire or I buzz you first."

Am replied, "Good luck, boss."

The hatch opened. Dante leapt down and into the dusty wind. Behind him, the shuttle rose into a power-saving, nearly silent hover. It could transform rapidly into an emergency escape or battle mode.

Otherwise, the lot and the ruins surrounding it were quiet, but the sounds of the not-so-distant battle were loud and unmistakable. Gunfire *crackled* and pulsecore rounds let out their distinctive high-pitched *fwoop* as they detonated. Metal *clanked,* and men shouted.

Dante's warrior mind registered the sounds of the battle for distance and constancy, but his energies stayed concentrated on the business of infiltration.

He went around the wall's far side, moving low to the ground, his boots making hardly any sound. Viv had once told him that when he was "on" in full Marauder mode, he reminded her of a cat stalking its prey.

Around the corner of the wall was a broad street. There was a chain-link fence, but most of it had collapsed, or the Dirtwalkers had cut it. The air grew thick as a wall of orange and green dust bore down on the battle scene. The metallic-tasting wind was a steady moan interspersed with whistles as the gusts slipped through cracks in the ravaged city.

Dante saw motion. He threw himself behind a concrete cylinder, his lean frame vanishing despite the gear he carried as a humanoid figure emerged from a mostly intact outbuilding on the other side of the street. A guard post for the alloy processing facility, perhaps.

There was no reason to assume that anyone in this place was friendly. He hadn't had time to get a good look at the person, but Dante intended to treat them as an enemy. Giving them the benefit of the doubt might well be suicidal.

The sentry moved quietly but didn't seem to be making any effort to conceal himself. He walked straight across the pothole-strewn asphalt, headed for the corner Dante had rounded, which would bring him within spitting distance unless he changed course.

Dante waited, barely breathing. Adrenaline pumped through him. His muscles tensed, ready for the fight. It would only take one thing going ever so slightly wrong...

The guard paused a short distance from the post. Dante figured his approximate position from the dim shadow he cast on the street. Then he began to circle sideways.

A dire warning signal went off in Dante's head. Slaine had been right. The Harij, if indeed the man was one of them, were better disciplined and seemed more intelligent than most of their planetary brethren.

The chances of being able to knife the sentry before he could shoot were too slim. Instead, Dante slipped his pulsecore carbine into his right hand and crept around the cylinder in the opposite direction of the guard's movements.

Then he popped out from the far side, aiming the gun and firing in one smooth motion. He finished squeezing the trigger almost before he had visual confirmation of the target—a serious risk but necessary.

Pulsecore carbines were versatile by design. Most of them, Dante's model included, had a folding fore handle and retractable shoulder stock that could transform one instantly into a small rifle. They could also be fired one-handed as a large pistol.

Dante saw the guard for a split second before impact. A Dirt-walker beyond any doubt, skinny and oddly bent, but with wiry strength and rugged vitality. He wore a ragged balaclava that covered most of his head and face and similarly crude and tattered clothes, but he'd strapped a twentieth-century style bulletproof vest over his torso. He'd probably raided it from some derelict old stockpile. He carried a late-model assault rifle of Old World European manufacture.

If the man saw what was coming and knew what would happen to him, there was no time for him to react. The single pulsecore round struck him near the stomach and detonated instantly. The tiny projectile unleashed its unstable payload and blew a hole the size of the man's head through his torso. The bulletproof vest, designed to protect against mere lead projec-tiles, did nothing to stop it.

The sentry's jaw fell open as a hollow groan escaped him and the blast's impact knocked him flat on his back. He twitched in agony for two or three seconds before blood loss and massive trauma did their work.

The distinctive sound of detonating pulsecore echoed

through the abandoned streets, but the ever-louder howling of the wind quickly overcame it. Dante got to his feet and scanned the surrounding area, the carbine at low ready.

No one was around. Still, any other Harij near the facility had probably heard the shot. He sprinted across the street, took cover behind the guard booth, and peeked through the facility's fence. This fence was intact and well-maintained.

The place looked quiet, but a shadow was moving. It was barely noticeable as the daylight dimmed behind the thickening clouds.

Dante paused. He could try to ambush the next guard, or he could attempt a diversion. He decided on the latter. Pulsecore rounds were relatively quiet when fired due to the low-intensity tech that discharged them. The bullet's impact created most of the noise.

He aimed at a half-collapsed shop down the street and fired twice. The rounds detonated about a meter apart, raising a faint greenish glow in each place and filling the air with their shrill report.

Footsteps pounded, growing louder and more urgent. Two ragged figures appeared from deeper within the complex, rushing out with guns in hand toward the noise. If Dante's ruse had worked, they probably thought the battle with the Reapers was growing closer, and that stray rounds were making their way to the facility.

Unfortunately, Dante saw them for only a second or less and couldn't line up a clear shot, or he would've eliminated them. Instead, he slipped in through the unlocked gate by the guard shack and made for the doorway the two sentries had emerged from.

Shadows closed over his head as Dante padded into the corridor. There was a faint light somewhere ahead, but he could see almost nothing so far. He returned the carbine to its holster and crept ahead as fast as possible without giving himself away. If he bumped into any hostiles, he would deal with them in an up-close and personal—not to mention quiet—fashion.

As he drew nearer the end of the hallway, he saw a chamber beyond. It was some sort of office piled with loot and garbage by the facility's current inhabitants. What was surprising, though, was that the steady white glow he'd noticed earlier was coming from a functional electric light.

As far as Dante was aware, the Dirtwalkers didn't use electricity. They'd lost its secrets after the calamity that drove most of humanity to the Stations. They'd returned to the ancient ways of relying upon fire and the sun for illumination.

Someone occupied the room. Dante flattened himself against the wall in the darkest spot he could find as another Harij guard, lounging in a chair, got to his feet and looked around. The man held a loaded hunting crossbow in his hands. His attitude was of sullen annoyance.

He barked something, a name or two, probably those of the pair who'd gone out to investigate. He tensed as he received no answer and gave no indication of having seen Dante.

The guard crept into the corridor's mouth. Judging by his inferior weapon and slow way of moving, Dante guessed that he was among the less-respected of their warriors, hence getting stuck with rear-guard duty.

The Marauder waited, part of him itching to do what he must, but long years of experience taught him to be patient.

Again the advancing man said something, this time a complete sentence or two. A couple of the words sounded vaguely like French, but otherwise, it was unintelligible gibberish. There was a so-called "trade tongue" among the different tribes, which Dante knew well, but he didn't know this language.

The Dirtwalkers and the Skydwellers no longer shared a common language. The "trade language" was only good for basic commerce. It was a question of whether the Dirtwalkers were even fully human anymore.

Dante wasn't sure. He tried not to think about it. The only thing that concerned him for the moment was surviving long enough to complete the mission.

The man stepped right in front of him. He sensed the intruder's presence a split second before Dante lunged.

The crossbow discharged its bolt a hand's length or so away as Dante's fist slammed into the man's head. He squeezed the razorfist's mechanism and the crystal-edged blade hidden within the gauntlet shot out. The blade pierced the man's skull and sliced into his brain before automatically retracting.

The guard fell, instantly dead. Dante caught him by the shoulders before he could crash to the floor, grateful that his hand reflexively kept clutching the crossbow. He hauled the body into the same darkened spot he'd hid in and moved on.

By the light of the white electric lamp, he inspected the office. It was plastered with old, frayed, yellowing posters and filled with basic survival supplies of the kind the Dirtwalkers always needed: water, food, medicine, tools, and clothes. Dante found it odd that they would keep such important stuff close to the exterior rather than burying it deeper within the facility.

Then it occurred to him. The supplies were specifically for the guards, who probably lived here most of the time. Whatever lay within the complex's bowels was even more important. The secret source of their electric power, presumably.

He wondered, *Did they have any real comprehension of the value of the alloy processing center? Had the Harij, in their relative ignorance, destroyed the very treasure that Slaine wanted so badly?*

Dante pushed such thoughts far from his mind. Instead, he peered into a crate and was surprised to see old computer supplies. Useless at the moment. If the Harij could generate electricity, they might eventually get *some* usage out of Old World tech. The prospect was frightening.

He examined the charts on the walls and found one of them was a facility map. It was a rambling place, but near the center and underground was where the actual processing took place. Getting there wouldn't be hard unless someone or something lay in the way.

Following the map's guide, Dante started toward the facility's center. There should be a way to get to the underground levels from that point.

He hadn't gone far when he heard the sounds of the two sentries he'd diverted tramping back into the building.

Cursing mentally, Dante swung around into the perpendicular corridor. He moved faster than he would've liked. If he bumped into further resistance, he would have to neutralize it immediately, perhaps sloppily. Getting pinched between two foes at his back and more in front was to be avoided at nearly any cost, even for someone of his skill.

The central lobby area had patrols. Two pairs of Dirtwalkers, a man and a woman in each case from the look of it, were circling the chamber's edges with weapons in hand. Despite the large-scale battle outside, the Harij remained surprisingly committed to keeping their hallowed site secure. The other guards were still coming behind him.

Dante kept close to the wall. The Harij's power source didn't give them enough juice to light the hallways, only the major rooms. The shadows protected him. He got nearly to the end of the corridor when one of the patrols passed, blissfully unaware of him. He poked his head out and looked around for anything he could use.

Shockingly, sitting in the corner atop a pile of other old excavated tech was an Old Atlantican prototype cloaking device. The slight blue glow suggested that its Atlanticore crystal center was still functional.

Had he been religious, Dante might have considered it a miracle. Instead, he was content with a happy coincidence. Of course, not everyone would've been able to use such an opportunity the way he could.

Keeping low to the corner of wall and floor, he sprinted out of the corridor, made a beeline straight for the pile of gadgets, and seized the cloaking device right before the second patrol reached a point where they might be able to see him.

The cloaker was about the size of an older personal sphere, larger than the current generation but still not too big or unwieldy. It was small enough to fit under a good-sized garment.

The real trick was locating the "on" button. The Atlanticans of old had been fond of hiding them under other devices to protect them from accidental misuse or to confound their enemies. Dante's hand clamped around it, seeking a particular ridge carved with faint runic letters on one of the seams.

He found it and pressed. A latch flipped open to disclose a small button, which he slammed with his thumb. The crystal briefly lit up with a soft blue-white glow around him. Then the world took on the oddly translucent and shiny appearance it always had from the other side of a cloaking field.

The second patrol looked straight at him. The man and the woman stopped simultaneously. Within their hoods, their eyes glimmered in the white light, distorted by the cloaker's optical effects but evident. Their confusion was obvious. They looked at a place where they expected to see something but saw nothing.

Dante stood perfectly still. Then he slowly stepped backward toward the wall, moving around to the rear of the pile of tech objects to get out of the way of any bodies that might rush past. He slowed his breathing to little more than a soft pant.

The second patrol flagged down the first, and the two pairs exchanged a short string of barking conversation, with the second's members flailing their arms. Then the two guards from outside ran up, said something, and after a short argument, all separated to rush in different directions down the various branching hallways.

Dante allowed himself a deeper breath, then exhaled. He *might* have been able to kill them all with quick work from his pulsecore, but the risks would've been enormous. His luck was incredible. However, it wasn't only luck.

Old technology had fascinated Dante Shale since he was a child. In many ways, it had been his first love. He'd forgotten more about obsolete machines than many people would ever learn. When encountering unfamiliar ones, he could often puzzle out how to use them with a little time and effort, or at least figure out how to transport them to a true expert who *would* know.

He stepped out from behind the pile of gadgetry. In the center of the lobby was a stairwell leading down.

Now he would find out exactly what lay below ground that was so important.

CHAPTER SIX

Beyond the heavy steel door that opened onto the rest of the basement complex was an antechamber of sorts. It had probably doubled as an employee meeting room or something, but the Harij had found a far more creative use for it. It had become their power plant.

Some genius among the tribe had figured out that motion, friction, and magnets were potential energy sources and rigged two old bicycles to a crude generator. Wires snaked from it and disappeared underneath the wall where they must have hooked into the facility's minimal but effective lighting system.

The only problem was how to keep the wheels spinning. They'd solved the dilemma in the most old-fashioned way imaginable—slave labor.

A single guard, armed with an electric baton that he must have taken from one of Slaine's earlier, ill-fated expeditions, stood with his back to Dante and watched over the two bikes, which they'd bolted to the floor. Mounted on them were a pair of young adults with overdeveloped leg muscles, half-naked and sweaty from their continuous pedaling. Their features were subtly different from the Harij, and Dante suspected they were captured members of an enemy tribe. Two other enslaved people slept on piles of rags in the far corner. Their shift would probably begin when the pair currently powering the complex collapsed with exhaustion.

Repulsed, Dante charged down the steps. Silent as he was, he moved too quickly to sneak up on the guard, but the man had no projectile weapons, only his baton. He pivoted at the last instant, his bony face tightening with alarm, and lashed out with a ragged snarl. Since Dante remained cloaked, he was purely reacting to sound and motion, not to anything he could see.

Dante caught his inner forearm and pushed it away so the strike went wide and threw the man off-balance. Then, stepping in as the guard tried to claw at his face, Dante slammed the razorfist against the man's chest, side, and neck, gouging him badly each time. Burbling gouts of blood flowed freely. Suddenly squealing in horror, the guard fell back, his strength flagging as massive blood loss and collapsing lungs dragged him toward death.

Leaving him to his fate, Dante turned off the cloaking device. The bluish sheen vanished, leaving everything before him darker and dull. He looked at the enslaved people. They stared at him with wide eyes but kept pedaling. The shock of seeing a man materialize from thin air was probably too much for their labor-addled brains, especially given how superstitious many Dirt-walkers were.

He wanted to tell them that they were free, but that would be a mistake. They would only rush upstairs and get killed by the guards on the first floor. Instead, he dragged the dead guard into a closet, then waved vaguely at the pair of riders before raising a finger to his lips and slipping past.

Later, when he'd finished his work, he might be able to free them. Not that it would lead to any great upsurge of morality on Earth. Their tribe would probably do the same or worse to any captured Harij.

The whirring sound of the bicycles faded as Dante reached what had to be his destination. Then his heart sank.

Spread before him was what remained of an unambiguous industrial operation that could only have been for processing minerals. The floor was vast, and beyond it lay a shadowed crater or gorge in the earth, probably an excavation pit that had partially collapsed over the years. It had taken some of the equipment with it. Some mechanical crushers, conveyor belts, sorting machines, cleaning implements, various wheeled crates, and old forklifts had survived.

No humans operated it, though. It had all lain dormant for decades. Nor was there anything identifiable as a metal alloy. Stepping in and examining things more closely, he concluded that even the dust coating the equipment was nothing more than standard powdered rock. Slaine's description had suggested a smooth, shiny, metallic substance, not mistakable for regular granite or limestone.

"Shit," he muttered. "How the hell did Slaine know what it looks like when there's none of the stuff around?"

He advanced through the rows of machinery, looking for clues and samples of the alloy itself. A single electric light near the processing area's entrance was tied in with the power grid and flickered away. Halfway across the space, Dante found it too dark to see much. He pulled out his sphere, set it to glow and hover, and allowed it to follow him, bathing a circle about two feet across in soft white light.

There were a few pebbles and the like lying around. He inspected them but found that they were mundane pieces of the surrounding earth.

Coolheaded as Dante usually was, acidic rage and frustration were slowly building within him, bringing his hands dangerously close to shaking and making the skin bunch up on the back of his neck. Someone had screwed up the intel. Slaine had, in some fashion or another, been wrong.

Either this was the wrong facility, and they'd meant to direct the team to some other place in the city, or the alloy had been cleared out long before now. Dante wondered if the Harij had excavated the last of it and sold it off as trinkets or were stashing it somewhere else.

Alternatively, unsanctioned Reapers or Plunderers might have discovered the place and looted it before Slaine could finally mount a successful expedition. That raised the question of how they'd infiltrated the facility with the heavy Dirtwalker presence all around.

Then he looked up, and his illuminated sphere cast its light on a broad service doorway with a window in its upper central area. He dashed toward it and had to watch his step to avoid tripping over the wreckage of a couple of abandoned machines and an overturned wheelbarrow.

The barrier didn't have an obvious knob or latch when he reached it. Dante grabbed his sphere and held it up to the glass. The refracted light made it difficult to see, but it appeared that beyond the door lay a big, open storage area piled high with lumpy, irregular shapes.

Unprocessed minerals. The closest thing he'd seen to a jackpot. It could simply be whichever metals made up the alloy rather than the final product, but it was the best chance he had.

He ran his hands over the door, seeking a way to get through it, but there was nothing. It must have opened remotely via a switch or computer elsewhere on the main processing floor. If it was an electrical switch, getting it open would be easy. Otherwise...

Dante cursed under his breath as he thought of the Harij guards prowling aboveground. They might come down and search the basement level at any moment. He combed across the walls and other exposed surfaces through the chamber's entire back half, looking for anything he could use.

He found a lever in the corner, but it was dead. The switch

was damaged and refused to budge. It didn't appear to have any juice running to it—either an independent and now-defunct source had powered it to begin with, or any wiring that connected it to the rest of the facility's grid had gotten damaged over the years.

There wasn't exactly time to call an electrician and a survey team to locate the wiring and pull off the wall panels. Instead, Dante rushed over to the shelving set next to a desk where he'd seen some equipment.

"Yes," he sighed, seeing an old desktop computer that looked more or less intact. It might not work, but it was better than nothing. He located the tower and pressed the power button. Nothing.

He hadn't expected it to work. All wasn't yet lost.

Dante pulled the cloaking device from his coat. He squeezed his left hand to deploy the knife from his razorfist and used the blade's tip to pry open one of the panels on the gadget's side, exposing the bulk of the small, glowing blue Atlanticore crystal that gave it life.

The nature of the energy produced by Atlanticore wasn't identical to electricity, nor to anything else in nature. Scientists long ago had proclaimed it unique and referred to it under a special category of physics. Dante recalled wanting to read up on it more, but life got in the way. The important thing was that you could use it to activate virtually any machine that ran on electrical power. The chief danger was overloading the system.

Dante set the cloaking device on the desk next to the computer while he examined the tower and found its main electrical outlet. He cut the wires running to the cord and touched them gently to the crystal.

A blue spark leapt up. A brief smell of ozone filled the air, followed by a low humming and a slight vibration through the wires. A destructive surge was possible. He had no other choice. He tapped the "On" button again.

This time, the computer made a grinding noise. The monitor flickered to life and soon steadied to reveal the crude two-dimensional imagery on the flat, oversized screen. Dust rose as the tower's internal fan kicked on. He found the so-called mouse next to the keyboard and wiggled it to verify it worked.

Surprisingly, the computer didn't ask him for a password before it went to its main interface display. The people who'd run the facility back in the old days must have felt that anyone able to get this far already had the necessary clearance.

After a moment's search, Dante located an icon for "Storage Control." Clicking on it took him to another screen that was simply green code text on a black background. He had enough experience unraveling such things that he could probably hack through it given enough time, but he'd hoped for something simpler.

Then, from behind him and above him came a rushing cascade of frantic noise. Many pairs of stomping footsteps, gunshots, pulsecore explosions, screams, and the interminable *clanking* and *crashing* of metal echoed through the corridors. It wasn't merely the sounds of a Harij war band returning to base. It was the undeniable signature of violent combat.

Dante's hand went automatically to his pulsecore, and his head swung around, lips peeling back from bared teeth. "God *fucking* dammit, are Hyde's people attacking the facility? How stupid *are* they?"

He couldn't think of anything else that would cause the ruckus unless perhaps another hostile tribe that *also* possessed modern weaponry had chosen this exact moment to invade Harij territory. He was somehow inclined to doubt that.

Frantic but undefeated, Dante turned back to the computer and scanned the primitive lines of code, punching keys as needed with his free hand. Each time he tried to enter input, the machine took precious seconds to load the next line or page.

"Come on," he panted. "Just open the damn thing." As long as he *had* the alloy to begin with, he could protect it while he fought free of the coming clusterfuck. If he got involved in a running gunfight while the door remained sealed, his chances of success plummeted with disturbing quickness.

Then the approaching tidal wave of noise and chaos reached the hallway outside the processing floor, and someone kicked open the doors. Dirtwalkers streamed in, a good dozen of them, with others making a fighting retreat to cover them. They fired guns of various types in the other direction down the hall while bullets and pulsecore rounds sailed back at them, taking a heavy toll.

Dante dropped to the floor. There was no way to stay out of the fight now. Getting the alloy would come only on the other side of neutralizing the enemy. Hiding behind one of the derelict machines, he pulled out his carbine, deployed the front grip and stock to better wield it as a rifle, and prepared for full-on battle.

A pulsecore round streaked past one of the Harij and detonated while grazing his upper shoulder. The high-pitched explosion tinted with green light tore the man's arm off and vaporized most of his neck, collapsing him in a shower of blood. The other Dirtwalkers, who seemed to be an even mixture of men and women, ignored it and fired back.

As the mangled body struck the floor, an electronically augmented voice bellowed, "Ha, ha, ha! We got them cornered. Finish off all the men!"

Dante's brain immediately fixated on Hyde's choice of words. He wanted the women alive. Before he could untangle the Reaper's motives, though, the first wave of retreating Harij came close enough that they'd see him within five to ten seconds.

No time. He couldn't risk it. He leaned out, aimed, and fired four shots in quick succession. The pulse rounds annihilated the first three Dirtwalkers, all blown off their feet before they realized someone was shooting at them from within the processing chamber.

Two others pivoted in Dante's direction, snarling, and one armed with a vintage submachine gun sprayed lead in the Marauder's general direction. Dante had already dropped back behind the heavy equipment. It stopped or deflected the bullets, but the noise was painfully intense, and bits of shrapnel raked his legs.

Then it seemed that Hyde's team finished off the main resistance in the hall and breached the processing floor before the Dirtwalkers could attempt to fortify their position properly. Boots stomped, weapons fired, and human beings screamed their death agonies.

Dante seethed with rage. There was no good reason why this should be happening—Slaine had made it clear that the Reapers were to keep the fighting *away* from the facility, diverting and minimizing the violence. Instead, Hyde had done the complete opposite. Dante looked forward to reporting to the executive that his chosen hatchet man was even more unstable and stupid than Dante had thought.

But not yet. The battle wasn't over. If a mass shootout was unavoidable, Dante was at least glad that it was happening on terms favorable to his side.

As pulsecore rounds detonated around him, though, he realized how precarious his situation was. Those explosions could destroy his cover far more effectively than a conventional bullet could. Hyde might even be moronic enough to throw in a grenade or two.

Ascertaining the positions of the remaining Dirtwalkers by sound and shadows, Dante spun and rose to a kneeling position, aiming at the fighters closest to him. One saw him instantly and nearly put a rifle round through him, but Dante squeezed off a shot that blasted the man's face apart a split second before. Another behind him went down under the carbine's barrage.

"Hey!" Mr. Hyde called. "Is that Shale? Are you back there?" His voice somehow carried through the cacophony of gunshots.

Dante dove behind a heavy cart as another Dirtwalker tried to get a bead on him. "Yeah," he shouted. "It's me. You're not supposed to be here." He peeked out around the cart's edge. The Harij were all but doomed. Only seven or eight of them were still fighting, whereas Hyde had at least two dozen of his troops with him. Others among the Dirtwalkers—mostly women—had surrendered and were being detained in the rear corner.

Hyde didn't respond to him. Instead, the cyborg stormed through the doorway toward a Harij fighter whose rifle had jammed. His awful voice reverberated as Hyde's half-mechanical hand clamped around the man's larynx, crushing it in the same motion as he lifted him to hurl over the safety railing into the darkened quarry beyond.

Dante had a clear shot at another of the dwindling resistance, but he hesitated. Hyde's men no longer needed his help. Once they neutralized the Dirtwalkers, Dante would be alone and cornered by the Reapers.

They wouldn't dare make a move against him, though. His crew would know, and the scandal would work back to Slaine himself.

Two more Harij died under a pulsecore barrage. There were only three more still holding weapons, one of them a woman. At last, they dropped their firearms and raised their hands, gibbering for mercy in the planet's rough trade language.

Dante barked, "Hold your fire. We won."

The Reapers stopped shooting. Hyde, turning away from the pit, gave Dante a disgusted glare, then stomped over to his men. Dante was about to explain the situation with the minerals locked behind the remotely-sealed door, but he never got the chance.

Hyde ignored him and waved one of his hydraulic arms as he growled, "Get all those women back to the other room for o-harvesting. Then we're done here."

His men wasted no time. They seized the surviving female

Harij, bound their hands with lockstrips, or simply paired up to carry them back into the hallway, one man holding their shoulders and the other their ankles. The mercs who remained pinned the male captives to the floor. Before Dante could protest, they executed them.

Dante's jaw dropped. "What the hell are you doing? This wasn't part of the goddamn arrangement, Hyde! *O-harvesting?* Are you fucking crazy? Are you trying to get Slaine to fire you? Recall that order!"

He held his carbine at low ready, eager to put a couple of pulse rounds right into Hyde's gaping mouth, but knew he was probably a dead man if he did. Hyde's crew might have mostly been cynical soldiers of fortune, but killing their commander didn't seem wise.

Hyde turned his head so slowly, and the room had fallen so silent aside from the fading screams of the Harij women that Dante heard the faint humming of the machinery that punctuated his every motion.

Dante's nostrils flared. "What you're doing is illegal," he pointed out.

Eduardo H. Curtidor snorted, the sound like an engine blasting air through a rusty duct. "I don't care."

CHAPTER SEVEN

Dante's finger twitched, desperately wanting to curl around the trigger of his carbine. He had a clear shot at Hyde's back.

When most of humankind had first abandoned their native planet to live in the elevated Stations, closer to the stars, many scientists and doctors had tried to draw attention to the potential hazards of existing in space. Those who designed the Atlantica Stations had done so with the utmost care and concern for the species' wellbeing, at least according to their knowledge and abilities.

Over the decades, as people had tried to adapt to a lifestyle amid wholly artificial conditions, certain complications had emerged.

In the first generation, people had been too busy fighting, working, and otherwise struggling to survive, but many had tried to raise families anyway. Still, it was mainly after the Stations were well established and relative peace and prosperity began to spread that people expected the baby boom to come.

It never did. Human fertility had, for reasons not yet fully understood, decreased during the transition to life in space. In particular, many women's bodies didn't produce enough eggs to allow pregnancy to occur. If they did, they would be unhealthy or warped and would result in miscarriages at best. The population plateaued and began to decline.

Some blamed the fertility crisis on obscure effects of the gravitech used to anchor the Stations and ensure everything remained in conditions comparable to the gravity found on Earth. Trying to recreate normality in one respect forced them to do profoundly *abnormal* things with risky and experimental technology. Some research had suggested that gravitech might indeed have been partially to blame despite concerted and well-funded campaigns by the tech companies to suppress the information.

Others thought that the weakening of human egg cells was more likely due to the increased consumption of lab-grown food. Or the related changes that had taken place in agriculture once they were raising all the crops with recycled water, different wavelengths of solar radiation, and synthetic fertilizers. In that case, too, evidence existed but wasn't entirely conclusive.

Finally, some individuals postulated that in abandoning their true home, the Atlanticans had contracted a kind of spiritual sickness, robbing the species of the will to reproduce. Deep down, they knew the Stations weren't the world meant for them. Such ideas couldn't be subjected to meaningful scientific testing but remained popular with a certain more superstitious or occult-oriented segment of the population.

What was undeniable, though, was that some women or couples desperately wanted children yet couldn't have them... Unless they were willing to pay substantial sums of money to do things that most of polite society regarded as abhorrent. Laws were passed. Bans and punishments were handed down.

Despite this, there was always a black market, and the process of ovary harvesting had flourished. By some strange miracle, the women of the old and broken Earth didn't suffer the same problems as those of the Stations. They were as fertile as any human beings born in the times before the planet's core had begun to die.

Dante's attention snapped back to the present as a couple of the mercenaries stepped casually in front of the doorway, blocking the Marauder from pursuing Hyde.

"Mr. Shale," one of them said in a dull, affectless tone. "It wouldn't be a good idea to make anyone too angry. We've got our orders. Let's all be realistic here. Nobody's going to blame you, anyway."

Dante glared at the man, his lip curling. "It isn't just about who gets the blame, jackass. Get out of my way. No, I'm not going to do anything stupid. I want to *talk* to your boss. He's such a reasonable man, after all."

The trooper hesitated, and the guys beside him also looked doubtful. They were probably considering their chances of survival if things went south and Dante decided to cut through them. He might not make it, but he was confident in his ability to take several of them with him to the underworld.

"Fine." The man who'd spoken first sighed. "Don't get your hopes up, though. There's a lot of money riding on this shit. As usual."

Dante wondered how much, exactly. And if it was less than, or greater than, the money Slaine had promised him for the alloy.

The guards stepped aside, watching Dante closely but doing nothing to stop him as he stormed through the doorway out of the processing area and turned right down the hallway. He had a feeling that Hyde intended to carry out the o-harvest as soon as possible, and probably in the room where the enslaved people had been pedaling the wired-up bicycles.

The hallway was mostly empty. Aside from the men who'd remained in the back chamber, everyone else had relocated to the bike room. At first, all Dante saw were the backs of half a dozen mercs near the corridor's mouth. Then he glimpsed the commotion of thrashing bodies between their legs or shoulders. Female voices shrieked and cursed.

"*Hyde!*" Dante shouted as loudly as possible. He didn't merely want the others to hear him. He wanted to overwhelm every other sound in the building. "Stop it right now. No o-harvesting until we contact Slaine and ask *him* what he thinks of this."

The Reapers turned to look at him, faintly uncomfortable but otherwise unimpressed. Dante ignored them and strode forward until he could push between the two men closest to the threshold's center and burst in on the scene taking place in the room beyond.

Hyde was there, along with all of the captives. Not too surprisingly, the Reapers had also laid claim to the two enslaved women and killed the males, piling their bodies carelessly in the far corner. The women all struggled in terror as the mercs pinned them to the floor, face-up, and Hyde watched with a leer of entertainment.

At the mouth of the opposite hallway were two men with portable gyno-extractors. The devices were supposedly "humane"—according to the manufacturers, they administered a local anesthetic while they sucked a woman's ovaries out of her body through her skin. Dante supposed it was...nice...of the designers to think of such a touch, given how the black market profiteers used the damnable things.

He pushed the bitter and cynical thoughts out of his mind and focused on Mr. Curtidor.

Hyde looked up as the Marauder approached. "I heard you the first time, Shale. You're stupider than I thought if you can't remember what I said two minutes ago. Don't bother calling Slaine. He won't give a fuck about anything you have to say."

Dante's eyes blazed as he stared at the huge man's barely human face. "Bullshit. I'm calling your bluff. We're contacting Slaine right now. This is illegal. Just go with the money for the alloy sample. You could help with that instead."

Hyde stared at him as though he'd said something utterly moronic or completely insane. Then he threw back his head and laughed, the augmented tones of his harsh, loud voice sending unpleasant vibrations through the walls and ceiling.

Before he could explain what was so funny, more figures jogged down the opposite hall. Three of them. Despite the lack of illumination, Dante recognized them instantly by their silhouettes.

His emotions went to war with each other at once. Part of him was angry that his crew would take such a massive risk in disembarking to come after him. They were now in the same potential shitstorm as he was, and their shuttle was sitting or hovering unattended in the lot across the street.

The other part of him was grateful. His confidence in his ability to intimidate Hyde's entire force single-handedly wasn't as firm as he was trying to make it seem.

"Explain," Dante snarled. "Explain why you thought this was a good idea and what's so goddamn funny."

He looked at Vivica, the first of his crew to emerge into the light, and nodded to calm her worried look. "They're trying to make extra money off o-harvesting because they want to destroy their reputations. I'm trying to talk them out of making an extremely stupid mistake."

Viv paused. Then Ambrose and Desiree came up behind her, wearing tightly drawn expressions of concern. On the plus side, all three were armed.

Hyde's roars of laughter lowered to a gurgling growl, the subsonic waves of his voice augmentation setting everyone's short hairs on end. He looked straight at Dante with an expression of loathing. It reminded him of a child who intended to torture a bug before killing it.

"Nobody cares about the alloy, Shale," he declared. "It probably isn't there. God, you're stupid. It was a cover story to get you to play along. The ovaries are the real prize, okay? Are you getting it now?"

Dante stared back, maintaining his frosty and unflappable expression through sheer force of will. He didn't think Hyde was bluffing this time. If what he said was true...

Hyde sneered. "Sooner or later, we would've told you. We figured you'd act like this, but you weren't supposed to be *right here* when we did the deed. What's that saying? No plan survives a fight with the enemy or something?"

One of the other mercs corrected him. "No plan survives *contact* with the enemy."

Hyde twisted his head to narrow his eyes at the man before looking back at Dante. "Yeah, whatever, you pedantic fuck.

"We *planned* to keep the Dirtwalkers busy outside and round up the women out there when we finished with them, but they disappointed us. Didn't expect them to bitch out so quick. They all ran back into their little hidey-hole here, so we followed them. The rest is history. Literally history since I'm pretty sure we wiped out the entire Harij tribe. They're past-tense now." He chuckled at the thought.

Dante's jaw clenched. His vision narrowed in focus. He saw only the cyborg formerly known as Mr. Hydraulic, and beyond him, a vast distance away, Cormac Slaine. Not even SSS would escape his wrath if they'd used him to do *this* kind of dirty work.

The Marauder looked briefly at his friends' solemn faces, then back at Hyde. He raised his left hand, sheathed in its razorfist, palm outward.

"This is where it stops. This is where you let these women go, take the other loot to make up for it, and back me up in reporting Slaine for violation of the Londonburg Black Market Act.

"I don't care how rich and important he is. I also know *you* don't care about doing the right thing. I think you might at least care about doing the *smart* thing. If you're too much of a goddamn animal to grasp that..." He raised his pulsecore rifle enough for the hulking cyborg to see the motion. "We're going to have serious problems."

The two mercs with the gyno-extractors had moved in and crouched beside the nearest of the captive women, whose strength was flagging as other men knelt on their shoulders and legs. Realizing that Dante's threat was entirely sincere, they stopped. The other men looked up from whatever they'd been doing and gripped their weapons. Gun muzzles drifted toward Dante's legs.

Dante stood still. This might be the last minute of his life. He'd been in many such situations before, never sure if luck, skill, and dumb courage would be enough to keep him alive. He wasn't certain now. Still, he'd decided on his course of action and wouldn't alter his stance.

"Yeah," Hyde grunted. "Right, 'smart thing.' I'm not surprised you would pull something like this, Shale. Trying to get yourself killed to protect a few random organs from Dirtwalkers whose names you don't know." His dull leer broadened into a toothy grin. "I hoped you *would* react like this."

Dante didn't flinch from the naked animal brutality on the bigger man's face. "You want to go?" His voice was quiet, the way it often got when he was deadly serious. "Is that what this is about? You think this is between you and me?"

"Ha," Hyde scoffed. "It's between your reputation and real life. It's about you thinking you're the best thing since gravitech because ooh, ahh, you escaped some Dirtwalkers on a couple of occasions. We all do that shit every time we go Dirtside. Wow, amazing—you put down a few Reapers who came after you. Low-grade guys, or middling at best."

For once, Hyde said something Dante agreed with. The reputations of some of the men he'd killed over the years exceeded their actual abilities.

Hyde went on, his voice louder and the words coming faster as he worked himself into a frenzy. "You think you're *Hombre*

Macho Último solely because you ghosted the Krieger Twins' bull-shit operation?" He gestured at his men. "Half of these guys could've done that with a little intel and decent gear. You think putting down Red Grin makes me think twice about your exis-tence, *pendejo*? All your belt notches are people I would've *stepped on.*"

Dante remained still as a titanium statue, aside from the gentle movements of his nostrils and chest as he breathed steadily. It wasn't much of a surprise that Hyde saw him as a rival, that the overgrown psychopath figured that Earth and Atlantica were too small for both of them. A drunk guy at a bar had once said that Mr. Hyde was possibly the greatest Reaper of their time. Dante wondered if Hyde had heard that. If so, it must have gone to his head.

"Would have," Dante repeated. "You've been out of that game for a long time now, haven't you? You stepped away from it, and you're a respectable professional now. Or at least, you will be if you prove that you're smarter than I think you are."

Slowly, deliberately, making no effort to hide what he was doing but without being sudden about it, Dante raised his gun and pointed it directly at Hyde's face. Everyone tensed, watching, but they sensed that Dante was giving the Reaper chief one last chance.

Dante's gaze focused beyond his target on the incongruous trio of his crew. He'd expected their solidarity. He'd anticipated that Viv, Am, and Des would recognize there was no turning back from this moment and would raise their weapons to back him up. Hopefully, that would bluff Hyde and his men into taking the path of least resistance, then laugh the whole thing off later as though it had been no big deal.

They didn't. They only stood where they were like nervous herd animals, watching and waiting in passive trepidation.

Part of Dante's heart sank. He tried to ignore it. His vision returned to the ugly visage of Eduardo Curtidor.

Hyde casually glanced over his shoulder at Dante's crew. Seeing their demeanor, he chortled at once, the sound disturbingly soft. Then he turned back to Dante, his face settling into a smile that somehow looked friendly without possessing the slightest trace of human warmth.

"Slaine Solar Solutions was willing to pay out the ass for the best, most expensive Marauder in all the Stations to handle this job. Weren't they?" His voice rose again in volume and ferocity, its metallic echo dominating the room.

"Of course, everyone can imagine the kind of money to be made on this particular o-harvest. It would have to be more than enough to cover your fee, Shale. Assuming no one gets in the way, there's no damn reason why we can't all take a sizable bonus on top of what we get for the job itself. *All* of us."

It was uncanny to hear the man sounding almost reasonable, to listen to words that were perilously close to sanity emerging from his hideous half-metallic face, articulated through the obscenity of his bestial yet artificial voice.

Uncanny, because he was recommending an insane and unreasonable course of action to Dante's crew, whom he trusted with his life.

Dante shook his head. "There's no way they'll take your side. My people are loyal to me. All this nonsense ends right now."

Vivica looked straight at him with an expression of sad resignation. She was still a relatively young woman, and the fact that they'd all probably die in the coming fight must have weighed heavily on her.

"Yes, Dante." She sighed. "It does." She raised her pistol and aimed it not at Hyde or the Reapers but *him.*

Am and Des, armed with pulsecore carbines, did the same. Am avoided direct eye contact while Des looked sour and disappointed.

Dante stared and blinked. He thought of himself as a smart man, quick-witted, and able to adapt to changing situations without much difficulty. Yet his brain refused to process what had happened. His mind tried to reject what his eyes and ears had registered, and his conscious thoughts scanned and rescanned his short-term memory to find an error, a way in which what he *thought* had occurred had not.

No, there was no use. His crew had betrayed him.

At that moment, the first time in many years he'd failed to be one hundred percent alert to what was going on around him, Hyde saw his opportunity and took it. Dante's trigger finger couldn't fire the gun before the Reaper charged.

CHAPTER EIGHT

Hearing was the first of Dante's senses to register what was happening. The kind of servos that powered state-of-the-art body armor and augmentation implants whined excitedly as their owner kicked them into high gear. The sound's meaning and the desperate warning it implied splayed across his consciousness a fraction of a second before the rest of him could react in time.

His reflexes hadn't slowed as badly he'd feared. Part of it was automatic muscle memory. He pivoted to the side at the exact instant Hyde lunged forward with his arm outstretched, smacked aside Dante's carbine, and shouldered him hard in the chest.

His last-second reaction wasn't enough to dodge the attack altogether, but it was enough to blunt the full force. The gun flew from his hand, clattered to the floor, and stopped against the wall. The impact of Hyde's bulky, metal-sheathed shoulder knocked the wind out of his lungs and hurled him into the air. He sailed back, trying to pivot to roll more easily when he fell and twisted in midair toward the nearest of Hyde's mercenaries, who stood firmly near the edge of the rear hallway.

"Hey!" the man protested as Dante crashed into him. Dante

grabbed his gun—not a pulsecore, but a high-end assault rifle, which was probably the next best thing—and yanked it out of his grasp as they tumbled to the floor.

While the merc fell against the wall and allowed himself to collapse to get out of Hyde's way, Dante struggled to gain his bearings again quickly enough to bring the gun into play and get a clear shot at his foe.

After making his initial move, Hyde paused to reassess the situation once Dante slammed into one of his men. Dante highly doubted that he cared about the man. It was only because crude and animalistic as he was, Hyde was no idiot when it came to fighting.

Dante recovered faster than he might have guessed. The rifle's muzzle snapped up, and people behind Hyde ran or jumped out of the line of fire as the Marauder squeezed off a burst of six or seven rounds.

The bullets struck Hyde around the torso, flattened against his armor or ricocheted off, and drew sparks where they hit. Their high velocities and the sheer amount of energy foot-pounds they dumped against the man were enough to halt and stun him for a second or so, but that was all.

Dante sprang sideways, getting out of Hyde's reach and forcing the cyborg to adjust his trajectory if he wanted to lunge at him again. The other men, as well as his crew, fell back, drag-ging the captured women aside and making room at the cham-ber's center. No one tried to interfere in the fight.

Dante fired again, but Hyde was somehow out of the way fast enough that only a single bullet, maybe two, found their mark, and they did virtually no damage. The others punched holes in the wall behind him.

Oddly, Hyde had a pistol hanging by his side but made no move to draw it, nor did he ask for a rifle or pulsecore carbine from anyone else.

Dante emptied the rifle's magazine, aiming for his enemy's head, but Hyde simply flattened himself before springing up and clearing half the room in one bound. Dante hurled the empty rifle at him and spun, looking for his fallen pulsecore.

"No." Hyde guffawed. "No, you don't!" As Dante spotted his discarded gun, Hyde's hand seized his coat's back collar and twisted it so Dante couldn't wriggle free of it, then hurled him aside to crash into the center of the room.

Dante gritted his teeth in pain as he climbed to his feet. The impact had badly jarred his left arm and shoulder. He was now without a projectile weapon as the Reaper circled and advanced, hopping weirdly in counterintuitive directions and grinning through his unkempt beard.

Hyde's armored body was strong enough that even pulsecore rounds would've had a tougher time killing him than would be the case with an ordinary man. Nevertheless, the barrage of small explosions would've taken their gradual toll. Against old-fashioned lead bullets, he was all but impervious. Emptying two full magazines of them into a single weak point on his husk might have done the trick. That was all but impossible given the man's speed.

Despite his hefty size and ungainly profile, Hyde could move faster than most professional athletes at the peaks of their careers. The bizarre network of hydraulic and bioelectric improvements made to his body allowed his physical form to push itself to lengths that wouldn't have been possible otherwise. All his brain had to do was command it.

Yet there was nothing *natural* about the process. His movements were jerky and linear. He shifted position, adjusted his coordinates like the machine he effectively was, then lunged in a particular direction with explosive velocity. It was terrifyingly efficient, but everything he did lacked organic fluidity. This made it all the more nightmarish to witness.

"Come on," the cyborg rumbled and made beckoning motions. "Come here, little Marauder. They say you're good with a knife. I'll give you one free shot at me. If you don't put me down right away, I get to hit back. You won't like that, Shale."

Dante circled back to his pulsecore and flipped it up with his foot. Hyde plunged into him as his hand clapped around its grip.

The Reaper's fist knocked the gun aside again as Dante depressed the trigger. A single pulse round streaked past Hyde's armored ribs and exploded against the corner, shattering one of the overhead lights and knocking chunks of plaster loose. The room went darker, but at least one light was still functional.

Hyde raged, "Coward! Trying to shoot me in the back when I'm offering a fair fight?" Dante struggled to get free of him, but he punched the smaller man in the stomach, seized his shoulders, and slammed him into the wall. One of Dante's ribs cracked and the air was again forced out of his lungs, leaving him gasping in pain. Then Hyde tossed him to the floor.

"Fuck's sake." Dante panted. "You're toying with me. Might as well finish the job. There's no *fair fight* against a guy who's two-thirds machine, you moron."

He slowly rose to his feet, then squeezed his left hand. The blade shot out of his razorfist. He also had a small conventional knife strapped to his hip, but his coat kept it out of sight. "I'll take that free shot first, though."

Hyde smiled and stomped toward him. "Do it. See if you can kill me with that thing." His glimmering eyes focused on the blade that protruded from the gauntlet. He watched it carefully enough that his attention to everything else seemed to suffer.

Dante took two steps forward, coming within arm's reach. "This is a crystal-edged blade, Hyde. It can probably punch through your armor. You think there's no way you can lose, do you?"

Hyde said nothing, only smirked as he waited for Dante to strike.

Dante knew what he was thinking. He would shift his posture so the blade connected but got diverted into the thickest parts of his armor or only made a glancing cut on the flesh below at worst. It would give him bragging rights later to say that he'd been wounded, or almost wounded, by the great Dante Shale. Then, when the blade failed to kill him, he would crush Dante's skull.

There was only one thing to do.

Dante lunged without telegraphing his attack, plunging the razorfist straight toward Hyde's heart. His senses were so attuned to all that happened before him that everything seemed to proceed in slow motion. He pulled his punch simultaneously with Hyde's slight pivot to the right...

While his right hand, dangling out of sight, slipped the spare knife free and in one fluid motion, looped over Hyde's massive arm to plunge the regular steel blade directly into Hyde's eye.

The Reaper screamed. The short choking sound of alarm lengthened and rose into an outright wail, which his electronic vocal augmentations harmonized in a perversely pleasing way. Dante jumped back, barely evading a reflexive swipe of Hyde's fist as the huge man's other hand pawed at his face and pulled the knife out.

The bizarre lack of blood or ichor from the wound suggested that his eyes weren't the ones he was born with. Yet, his pain was real. Part of the bastard was still a human, made of mere flesh.

Still, the knife hadn't driven deep enough to kill him. It was Hyde's turn to hit back.

Dante turned and ran. He pushed through the line of mercenaries standing in front of the hall leading to the exit, who hadn't expected him to try and flee. He bolted past Viv, Am, and Des, who stared at him.

"Hey!" Hyde raged. "Get back here... Shoot him! Fucking kill him!"

The opening salvo of gunshots and pulse rounds came as

Dante sprinted up the stairs, weaving irregularly to make himself a more difficult target. The last thing he fleetingly saw before he emerged on the ground floor was Vivica aiming her pistol at him and firing.

Bullets and pulse detonations wrought havoc on the stone beneath his feet and off to his sides. Something hit him in the back, but he couldn't say if it was a pair of bullets or simply a chunk of displaced concrete. Dante hurled himself along the steps, caught the safety fence around the stairwell, and swung sidelong into one of the hallways. In his mad rush, he wasn't sure if it was the same one he'd entered by, but his sense of direction reasserted itself after a moment.

He was moving perpendicular to his original course into the building. If there was an exit somewhere ahead, it would drop him off closer to the site of Hyde's men's battle with the main Harij force. That could be either the best or the worst possible direction to go.

Worst, because Hyde had probably left a few men to guard the ship, who might spot him or shoot him on sight. Best, because it was the direction they would least expect him to take. If he was fast, he might slip unnoticed around to the empty lot from the back, get to the shuttle, and see if he could pilot the damn thing back to Londonburg by himself.

It had been a few years since he'd flown…before Ambrose had joined up. He had to trust himself to remember all the important stuff. The alternative was death.

The hallway was empty except for a couple of corpses—Harij sentries who'd been blasted to pieces by pulsecore. Dante hopped over them and headed for what looked like an external doorway. Behind him, he heard the whole force fanning out into the facility from the central room with the stairwell.

It occurred to him that there wouldn't be anyone to stop the Reapers from doing what they'd come to do. The ones not involved in the pursuit had probably already begun the harvest.

Dante reached the doors and flung them open. Beyond was a paved courtyard with dead trees in stone-lined basins and a fountain that contained only a pitiful trickle of brownish water. He ran its whole length and emerged near another section of fence that had warped enough for him to jump it with ease. His feet struck the asphalt, and he ran out into the street.

Now that he'd managed a decent head start on his pursuers, Dante took in everything happening outside, all around him.

The storm had arrived. Visibility was less than half of what it had been when they'd first arrived, with brown rust and pale ash blowing on the ever-stronger howling winds. Through the gaps in the ruined buildings, he faintly saw the empty field area where the main conflict had occurred. The storm made it hard to discern the details, but he estimated at least forty dead Harij lay there, with around half a dozen of Hyde's other men watching over the Reaper ship.

They didn't see Dante. There was no reason for them to expect him, and the dusty wind obscured their view. Dante looped left. There was enough jumbled detritus in that direction for him to duck behind it as he made for the lot's far side where hopefully the shuttle still hovered.

It occurred to him that he should've diverted course to the body of the first exterior sentry he'd dropped, the one with the rifle who'd emerged from the guard booth. It was too late now. Getting to the shuttle would be his only way of acquiring a gun.

He ducked behind a pile of rubble as the wind brought the barking voices of Hyde's men to his ears. It sounded like the bulk of them would head straight for Dante's ship, but a handful would spread out in other directions to be safe.

Dante spotted the fence around the lot, vaulted over it, and gazed with an almost overwhelming sense of relief at their shuttle. *His* shuttle.

The two men Hyde had posted there turned and immediately opened fire with their pulsecores.

"*Shit*," Dante rasped, his body twisting and nearly trying to jump out of its skin as he struggled away from the faint streaks of the explosive bullets. Two or three of them struck debris around him and launched clouds of sand and gravel into the air in tandem with the shrill signature of their blasts and the pale green light they produced.

With no real way to fight back, Dante was reduced to the stupidest of all possible options. Mindlessly, he fled deeper into the city, deeper into the ruins. The pair of guards came after him, taking carefully aimed shots as they moved and nearly killing him half a dozen times before he lost them—or so he hoped—in an especially ragged and desolate nearby slum.

Dante staggered down an alley, slipped through a hole in a broken wall, and huddled in a dark corner with an old pile of clothes or blankets. He collapsed against them, panting, but sprang up quickly. There was a body under that pile!

"Looks like we both got the worst end of this deal," Dante told the body. "At least your friends didn't turn on you. I hope." The pain of the betrayals competed with the pain from his various injuries. He was close to total exhaustion.

"Dude, this has been my biggest fuck-up in years. Have I ever learned anything?" Dante paused in his conversation with the body. "Please don't reply."

He ran his hands over his body and turned his mind to the task of sensing how well he functioned, feeling where the hurt was. He'd been involved in enough violence to assess his physical condition when he had to, but he was no doctor.

Notably, at least one of the things that struck him in the back on the stairs had been a bullet. It had ripped through his heavy coat, diverted by the thick fabric enough to have saved his life, but it still tore a chunk of his flesh out and might be lodged somewhere under the bottom of his shoulder blade. He would need a mirror to be sure. He was bleeding from that wound and various abrasions from the drubbing he'd suffered at Hyde's hands.

His face flushed with shame. Not many people could best him in hand-to-hand combat. Hyde had the obvious, unfair advantage of massive cybernetics, but it was still an agonizing wound to his pride that the monster Reaper had dominated him. He'd been *toying* with him, even. Dante probably owed his life to Hyde's sadism.

Aside from the gunshot, he didn't have any other injuries that seemed debilitating or life-threatening, provided none of them got infected. He felt around under his coat. He still had a small emergency medical kit. Not the more comprehensive one in his backpack, which he'd lost in the facility during the fight, but it was far better than nothing.

Dante opened it and poked around for things he could use. Good old-fashioned antiseptic cream and a couple of dermal seals, for starters. He applied some of the disinfectant to his back and awkwardly placed a seal over it. It sucked against the wound, closing it and stopping the bleeding. If the bullet was still somewhere in his body, removing it later might be an unpleasant business.

The basic kit also included two stimpacks. He *wanted* one now but decided to save it. As bad as things were, they could always get worse.

His team had abandoned him like Atlanticans had abandoned Earth. Used up and tossed aside. Now Earth was a savage land, made hostile to life, and the things that did survive here enjoyed no luxuries and no mercy. The people he might encounter wouldn't react to his presence with sympathy or hospitality. They would kill him for his boots or any other piece of quality equipment he carried on his person.

Other things would kill him for the more primal reason that he might taste good and they were hungry: Nightmutts and other horrifying creatures. At least the insects would more likely wait until he was dead. Dirtwalkers were relatively indiscriminate about meat sources when food was scarce—as it often was.

"Such a great place," he muttered. He drew a couple of careful breaths so he didn't irritate his cracked rib. "Wonder if I can still try to stow away." He dragged himself to his feet and crept out of the building via a naked doorway, looking around with caution before he exposed himself to anyone who might be watching.

The gusting storm partially muffled it, but Dante recognized the sound of a ship lifting off. He looked around and saw it. His. Viv, Des, and Ambrose were leaving. The shuttle grew smaller as it rose before being obscured by clouds and streams of blowing dust.

"What the hell, Am?" Dante panted. "He's seriously going to attempt a full ascent through this shit?" Granted, if they could get high enough unscathed, they'd simply leave the storm beneath them and have a smooth trip from there on. Still, the risk was substantial. Ambrose might have been merely moving the shuttle somewhere else—somewhere farther from Dante—to wait until conditions improved.

The Reapers didn't seem to have left yet. They probably had extra work to do securing their pilfered ovaries. Plus, a cargo-grade ship like the one they'd brought could potentially suffer worse consequences from flying in a dust storm than Dante's could.

Dante grimaced. Something filled him for the first time in a long while…a cold, deadly hatred. He contemplated throwing his life away for the chance to kill Hyde or some of his men. If there was no way for him to escape the planet, that might at least offer him some small, final satisfaction.

"No," he murmured. "Be smart. It's not over yet."

Ignoring the pain of his wounds as best he could, Dante went back inside to the body. "My friend, if I'm going to survive out there I need some help from you." He took the dead man's clothes, shook them out to dislodge stray critters, and recoiled at the blood-sucking insects that fell out. "Never mind." Dante's coat had seen enough adventures that it didn't look out of place. It would have to suffice to help him blend in.

The faint glint of metal caught his eye. The body had been half-covering a rifle. Dante picked it up reverently. "I promise to make good use of your weapon, my friend. Perhaps I can make up for my stupidity." He covered the body with the blanket that had been there and went back outside.

He climbed a barely intact staircase going up the exterior side of a three-story apartment building and crouched on the roof next to the stair shed, using it to shield himself from the worst of the winds. He waited, listened, and observed.

Within about five minutes, the storm began to abate. It would likely bluster on for another twenty or thirty minutes, but the worst of it seemed to be over. Visibility improved. Night was falling quickly, but there was enough daylight left to see most of what was happening nearby. Across the ruins, near the far end of the empty field, the Reapers were loading their precious cargo and preparing to leave.

Dante frowned, musing whether they'd killed the women after harvesting their eggs. They'd virtually annihilated the tribe regardless, but finishing off the last of them rendered helpless and unable to reproduce would've added insult to mortal injury.

With Dante himself unable to testify back at the Station, it would be easy to blame the atrocity on him. The true culprits could escape justice while directing any effort at vengeance at Shale, the fallen hero. He'd been so naïve.

Then something else caught his eye; subtle motions from deeper within the city, closer to the immense crater at the center from where Downtown Atlantica Metro had been excavated wholesale and lifted into space.

Dirtwalkers. A good-sized war band, probably from a rival tribe to the Harij. *Had they figured out that their enemies had been all but wiped out and were now moving in to scavenge the spoils?* Dante wondered. It was common for the savage peoples of Earth to do that any time some calamity befell their neighbors. Resources of any kind were too precious to waste on the dead.

If any of the Harij were still alive—a dozen women at most, perhaps, mutilated as they were—then the other tribespeople would kill them, rape them, or enslave them before they recovered from the ovary-extraction process. It was part of the way of life here.

"Damn." Dante rubbed his eyes and headed back to the staircase, clinging to the rail and hobbling back down toward the street. "Why do I care? I helped kill the bastards off. If we didn't wipe them out, the weather or the Nightmutts would have."

Technically, he owed the Harij nothing. Yet he couldn't think of a better way to spend his time, under the present circumstances, than to potentially give the tribe's wretched survivors some small measure of peace and mercy. If he was doomed, he liked the thought of going out fighting for a gallant-sounding cause like that. It was the next best thing to actual survival.

The raiders, the enemy tribe, whoever they were—they were coming in fast. Dante had a good head start on them, but being able to cut them off would require him to move more swiftly than he wanted to. His wounds were beginning to ache. His mind and muscles screamed at him to stop, rest, and deal with everything tomorrow.

"No," he grumbled. "We're doing this, and we're doing it *now*."

Hobbling as fast as he could down the empty, dust-blown street, he came to a mostly intact building that was a respectable four stories tall. Big enough that from the roof, he would be able to snipe as many of the interlopers as he had ammo for, at least until they wised up and fled.

The rival tribespeople were moving down a broad alley with masses of collapsed rubble on either side. It would allow them to take the most direct route toward the facility but limited their ability to dodge to the sides and disappear into the ruins since they would have to climb over large, dense piles of rough debris.

Dante kicked down the side door, whose hinges were mostly rotten and rusted anyway, and easily found the stairwell. The whole interior space was almost indescribably bleak and desolate but not as filthy as he would've expected. As he hauled himself up the four flights, he hoped none of the locks were in use.

He emerged without incident and rushed immediately to the appropriate edge, peering over while he caught his breath.

They would be within range in about a minute and a half. Dante propped his rifle up against the roof's surrounding half-wall and fished around for his medkit. There was no telling how well this little engagement might go. If the tribespeople didn't flee, they might well decide to besiege him, in which case it could be a fight to the death if there were enough of them.

Dante found one of the stimpacks and injected it. He felt the familiar rush of euphoria, the slightly nervous energy combined with manic enthusiasm, and paradoxically, clearness of mind.

"Right," he muttered and picked up the rifle. Daylight was almost gone. Had the enemy tribe arrived twenty minutes later, it might have been impossible to see them. In the current twilit gloom, they were little more than black silhouettes amid the dull browns of the ruined metropolis.

The rifle's front sight drifted up into the notch of the rear sights. He would kill for a scope or a red dot, especially with a nice night vision setup, but sometimes people had to make do with the low-tech option. At least he knew how to shoot with iron sights alone.

As the first of the raiders came into his line of fire, he sighted in the rifle. Then he felt cold, sharp steel across his neck.

He went totally still. His lungs were empty so breathing wouldn't interfere with his shooting, but now he allowed a slight inhalation through the nose. Then he moved his finger off the trigger and his hands away from being able to do anything threatening with the gun. His eyes turned sideways, and his heart sank.

The blade was crude but appeared to be of strong build, with an edge sharp enough that it tickled faintly. It might have already lacerated the topmost layer of his skin. He couldn't see a hand directly behind it, so it was probably a spear rather than a knife.

The blade moved away from his flesh—barely. The person wielding it was satisfied that he got the message and gave him a small margin to move. A grunted voice said something that might have been "up" in the Dirtwalker common tongue, but it was hard to be sure.

Dante slowly rose to his feet, let the rifle topple over to the roof, and tried not to wince at the prospect of leaving it lying there chambered and unsafe, but he had other more pressing concerns. He kept his hands up and spread, level with his shoulders. Then he turned to examine his guest.

There were several of them. Five that Dante could see clearly, plus others hovering behind or crowding near the threshold of the stairs that led back into the building below. All women.

The one out in front, holding the spear at his throat, was easily the most distinctive and frightening. She was tall and muscular with a lean hardness and an aspect of barely contained ferocity. Her dark straight hair was bound up to spill back over the crown of her head, and on her lean face were two scars, almost like tattoos. They formed a pair of crescents whose points touched the corners of her eyes at the tops and the crease beneath her lower lip at the bottom.

None of the other women looked like he should take them lightly either, even if they weren't as terrifying at first glance.

Dante looked into the lead one's black eyes and waited. The blade of her spear hovered in place, a finger's breadth from his jugular.

She spoke in the Dirtwalker trade tongue, enunciating her words well enough that Dante could understand her instantly. He was relatively fluent in the language, but the massive profusion of different accents and dialects occasionally made it hard to comprehend without a moment of digestion.

Not this time, though.

"Do not move, Moonfiend," she rasped, using her people's typical derogatory term for anyone from the Stations. "Or you will be Urshielle's first kill tonight."

CHAPTER NINE

Dante's eyes wandered to the cauterized wounds low on the women's torsos, the telltale scars that would forever mark them as having been subject to ovary harvesting. Supposedly the gyno-extractors performed their grim work with minimal pain and minimal tissue damage, but there was no way around the fundamental atrocity of what the devices did.

He then looked toward the housing around the stairwell, where the rest of the Harij women clustered and watched. "If you kill me, you kill them as well," he said to the lead spear woman, using the Dirtwalker tongue. "I'm here to save them."

The others' faces were stony, but a few blinked in confusion or frowned in distaste.

As for the big one—Urshielle, if Dante had heard her correctly—she made a faint breathy sound that might've been a scoff. "What? Save them, you say, Moonfiend? No. You're too late to spare the silver-scraped. You already knew that, did you not? I see you looking at the wounds on our bodies."

Dante wasn't the type to blush or flinch when accused of something that he knew was true. He only stared back flatly, thinking of the ravenous tribespeople below, streaming closer and closer.

"I can still keep them from being killed. I can help you survive what's coming. The warriors of another tribe are moving through the streets, coming for *you* and anyone who's still back at the facility. They saw what happened. With your people weakened and mostly dead, they're going to either enslave or kill you few women and take everything that once belonged to you. I was about to shoot the first of them when you ambushed me."

Urshielle held his gaze, unflinching. She raised a hand and motioned for one of the other women to rush to the roof's edge.

Looking over, the girl said, "Yes, it is true! They're almost upon us." Something changed in the demeanor of the others, an increase in tension, although Dante wasn't sure it could strictly be called fear.

The spear woman didn't look at them. Keeping her eyes on Dante, she mused, "Not all death is of the body. The people of the moon do not seem to understand this the way the people of the Earth do. Had I the time, I might teach you the different ways to die...but it would seem that right now, I have no time."

Another of the women, one perched at the threshold of the stairs, added, "We left six at the facility. They will not be enough to hold out by themselves."

"See?" Dante pointed out. "I have no time, either. Your deadly rivals are coming this way, and they'll be upon us in seconds. They'll find us up here, sooner or later, even if they pass us on their way to kill the six you left behind. If we can ambush them now, we can change that. Either help me or kill me, Urshielle—but either way, stop wasting my time."

The warrior took a step straight back. The spear went with her, but its point stayed aimed at his neck. She glanced over her shoulder toward the darkened streets below. "Very well, Moonfiend. If you would now save those you ravaged, show them your teeth."

"I didn't ravage anyone," Dante asserted. He picked up his fallen rifle, using a movement that was quick but smooth and steady enough to dispel the women's suspicion that he was about to fire on *them*. "And I'm not using my teeth until I'm out of ammo."

Urshielle smirked. "Good." Then, so swiftly that Dante couldn't react to it, she spun away from him, retracting the spear. The other women fell in behind her as all of them piled into the housing and descended the stairs.

"Wait," Dante protested, but he knew it was useless the instant the word left his mouth. He sighed and turned back to the roof's edge. The approaching enemy tribespeople were almost directly below him, and he wondered if they'd heard his and the Harij women's voices.

He saved his cursing and grumbling for later, assigning it to a portion of his mind that would lay dormant until the coming danger was past. *Why were they going downstairs?* he wondered. It would've made more sense for them to wait while he picked off some of their foes with his rifle, then defended their elevated position atop the building if the Dirtwalkers tried to assail them.

He imagined the women were concerned about their fellows, back at the compound and largely defenseless. They must have figured that attacking the other tribe from the rear while Dante fired on them from above would pin them down, distract them, and give the women still languishing in the facility time to prepare and arm up.

The best thing he could do for them was thin out the opposition on the ground. He shouldered the rifle, spotted the nearest of the scuttling dark shapes below, and focused on the front sight, lining it up as he exhaled and curled his finger around the trigger.

The first shot split the air like a descending thunderclap. The night had grown almost uncannily silent since the dust storm abated, and the gun's report was unnaturally loud. It echoed throughout the ruins, the sound waves likely traveling to the depths of the vast crater where the bulk of Atlantica Metro had once been.

The Dirtwalker unlucky enough to be in the line of fire appeared to jump forward before twisting sideways, his ragged body oddly motionless before a spasm went through him and he died against a pile of rubble.

His companions knew the sound of rifle fire well. They flung themselves aside, pressed against walls, ducked into alleys, or sought cover or concealment behind heavy dumpsters and the engine blocks of burned-out car shells.

Dante noted with grim annoyance that the episode with Urshielle had allowed the hostile tribe to proceed to an area with more things to hide behind. Had he been able to start shooting when he originally planned to, the Dirtwalkers would've been sitting ducks.

He still had the drop on them. They didn't yet know exactly where the shot had come from. Two of them crouched near the base of a ruined building, frantically looking around for the sniper. They'd made themselves into smaller targets...but they were still targets.

A man and a woman, Dante decided, based on what little he could see. Among many Dirtwalker tribes, it was common for women who were old enough and not engaged in rearing children or other essential tasks to join the men on raids. The rigors of survival on Earth were such that they appreciated any extra sets of hands. Since both were participating in an action that Dante had sworn to disrupt and destroy, both were fair game.

The woman was the smaller of the two, so he targeted her first while she was unmoving. The iron sights drifted over her head, and Dante squeezed the trigger. A dark stain appeared on the building wall behind her, and she fell over as though a flipped switch had turned her off.

The man sprang to his feet before the gunshot echoed. He

moved closer to Dante's position to get to the mouth of an alley. Dante had expected as much. He only had about a second and a half to make the shot. It was enough. His next round took the man somewhere in the midsection, knocking him off his feet and leaving him twitching on the ground.

Before Dante could get a bead on the others, someone shot back. He saw only a single flash from the darkness within the same alley the man had run toward, but at least two or three bullets smacked into the building's upper reaches. One blew a chunk of concrete from the wall only a foot from Dante's elbow.

He retracted the rifle and fell behind the barrier, his mind fixing the details of the scene below in place, so he would know which areas to keep an eye on when he rose. He crawled about three meters to his right. That way he would have a slightly better angle from which to shoot the tribespeople out in front, the ones closer to the facility. The Harij women would probably be emerging below at any second to deal with the tribe's rear echelon.

When Dante popped back up with his rifle shouldered, his heart sank. The invaders had divided their force, with half of them scampering off toward the compound. He had no good shots at any of them, but he fired one round into their midst regardless. There was an off chance he might hit someone. The point of impact would be closer to the facility, increasing the likelihood that the women within knew that something was wrong and were preparing accordingly.

Then Dante swept the gun sidelong and examined the street closer to himself. The other half of the raiders were converging on the building. They'd figured out where he was and were determined to dislodge him. He took a shot at one of them across the street but was too hasty and missed by a hand's breadth. "Dammit," he rasped.

Directly beneath him, the doors burst open. The Harij women sprang out, screaming a war cry in unison and engulfing the first two of the attackers. The others returned the cry, roaring and charging into battle.

He was a pretty good marksman, but there was almost no way Dante could've fired into the tangled mess beneath him without a good chance of hitting the wrong people. Grimacing, he pulled back and turned to the stairwell's housing.

He would have to go down and deal with things in a more up close and personal fashion. No avoiding it.

As he marched toward the stairs, he peered at the rifle's magazine. It was difficult to tell in the dark, but he estimated by using the small window holes that there were only two or three rounds left in it. He hadn't expected it to be full when he'd started. Bullets were a precious commodity.

No one challenged him on the fourth floor or the third, but he heard the sounds of combat below him. Some of the raiders had broken through the Harij's front line and were probably making for the staircase itself. Dante held his rifle ready to fire, but he kept his finger straight to the side to avoid accidentally shooting one of his allies if she should surprise him.

He approached the second-floor landing. The doors crashed open, disclosing four people. One Harij woman fought a hopeless battle against a trio of invaders, two men and a woman.

Dante's reflexes responded instantly. One male was out in front with a pistol, an old nine-millimeter model. He raised it, but not quickly enough. Dante shot him twice. The first round shattered his hip, knocking the man off-balance and ruining his shot, but not dropping him. The second shot went straight through the middle of his chest. A spout of blood pulsed from his back and he fell over without a sound, dead.

As the other man struggled with the Harij woman, dragging her back through the doors—Dante heard her scream and assumed the worst—the female raider hastily fired a hand crossbow at him. He pivoted and barely dodged the bolt.

The woman drew a long knife and charged up the flight of

steps, her stringy hair bouncing against her shoulders. Dante aimed and pulled the trigger. Nothing happened. The magazine was empty.

He spun the rifle in his hands and swung the butt at the woman's head. It connected at a glancing angle. She stumbled sideways but grabbed the gun in both hands, dropping her knife the better to attempt to twist it out of Dante's grasp.

Since she didn't weigh much, Dante simply picked her up and threw her over the railing. Her face went taut with alarm as she tumbled into the musty darkness at the center of the stairwell. The rifle came loose from his grasp, remaining in her hands, not that it would do her much good. She *thudded* to the ground floor below a second later and didn't move again.

There was still one more to deal with. Dante rushed down to the corpse of the first man he'd shot, his hands going straight for the pistol. He fumbled the weapon out of the dead hand's grip right as the third raider reappeared.

He was a broad-shouldered man with massive arms that contrasted bizarrely with his skinny waist and the ribs visible through his taut skin that showed under the rags he wore. His beard was ragged and patchy, and his eyes wild with animal fury. He held a makeshift spear that looked like a pole with a machete blade tied to it.

There was no time. Dante raised the pistol and squeezed the trigger as the big man's eyes focused on him. The weapon jerked in his hands, *cracking* once and filling the space with its ear-ringing report. The empty casing flew sidelong to strike the railing before plummeting into the open space.

His aim had been true, but the raider didn't react to being shot. When Dante pulled the trigger again, he got only a faint *click*. The man with the spear roared and charged. There was a slight trickle of blood running down his chest.

Dante tapped the bottom of the magazine and racked the slide in case it was simply a misfire, but no new round slid into the chamber. The gun was empty. Cursing without words, he flung it at the Dirtwalker's face.

It struck the man across the chin and cheek, doing no serious damage but making him flinch enough that his lunging strike went wide. The machete blade carved the air a few centimeters beyond Dante's hip.

Dante lashed out with his leg. His boot struck the man in the jaw, and he felt things crunch beneath it. At last, the big man reacted, halting and grunting in pain. Now was the time to finish him.

Deploying his razorfist, Dante moved inside the effective range of the raider's spear. The split-second hesitation the man might experience while trying to lift the weapon again could make all the difference.

The Dirtwalker proved smarter than Dante had hoped. He dropped the spear and reached out with his long, muscled arm. His hand wrapped around Dante's neck as the Marauder's crystal-edged blade was about to slide into his throat.

Dante reflexively pulled his hand back and stabbed the man's wrist, twisting the blade viciously. The raider's hand convulsed, squeezing his neck harder so Dante saw spots. Then the grip released. Dante sprang forward again, putting his weight behind the thrust and plunging the blade through the tall man's eye socket. He let out a short, sharp, choking cry and instantly went limp.

Gasping, Dante ripped the razorfist free and kicked the corpse aside. No one else was coming for him, but the battle was still raging on the floor below. Wood and metal *crashed* against each other, men and women growled and screamed, and bodies *thudded* against the floor.

He picked up the spear, retracted his razorfist, and checked his other knife. Fights with low-tech weapons were an incredibly ugly and dangerous affair, but it seemed as though both sides had exhausted their complement of projectile weapons. He had no choice. Whatever foes remained, he would have to deal with them hand-to-hand.

Beyond the second-floor threshold lay the dead body of the Harij woman who'd tried to resist the three invaders Dante had dispatched. He grimly shook his head.

After the short hop to the final intermediary landing, Dante swung around and charged down the final half-flight of stairs. He kicked open the door beyond and emerged into the lobby in a defensive stance with the crude slashing spear held ready.

To his mild surprise, only four people still stood. It had sounded like far more from above. Three of them were Harij women, and only one of the attackers remained. The instant Dante saw him, the invader backhanded one of the women aside while the other two braced themselves. All four carried various styles of makeshift swords or large knives.

Dante rushed the man as he sprang at the women. The two defenders crossed swords to repel his strike, and by the time the raider grasped what was happening, Dante had buried the point of his spear in the man's side. He gasped, eyes bulging, and tried to pull away. The two Harij battered his weapon aside and hacked into his neck, face, and stomach with frantic blows.

As the man collapsed and the woman he'd knocked down rose to her feet, Dante's gaze rose and scanned the rest of the lobby and the increasingly pitch-dark city beyond the broken windows. "The facility," he barked, directing his voice at the three women without looking at them. "Did the others go back there?"

The one who'd been backhanded grunted, "Yes."

It sounded like she might have more to say, but Dante didn't give her a chance. He picked up another crudely made short sword from a nearby corpse and held it in his left hand while keeping the spear in his right. Then he burst out of the building, onto the street, and headed toward the compound.

He couldn't see much. His eyes were adjusting to the darkness, but Dirtside nights often had a smoky and oppressive quality that exceeded what Atlanticans were used to. In space, even the surrounding blackness was often curiously bright as long as nothing obstructed the sun.

He passed three or four corpses along the way and didn't stop to check if they'd belonged to the Harij or their enemies. If Urshielle and the others were trying to defend the women they'd left behind on their home turf, they would need help immediately. The compound offered many ambush spots but little high ground.

As Dante reached the half-collapsed fence, an awful wave of fatigue welled up and threatened to overwhelm his consciousness. The stimpack he'd injected helped some, but it couldn't completely defeat the basic fact that he was close to total exhaustion. He was lucky he'd avoided taking any major wounds.

He neared the front entrance of the facility's main building. Somehow he'd assumed the hostile tribe would attempt a direct assault, knowing that their foes were currently weak. He'd expected them to try to swarm them and achieve victory through speed, surprise, and brute force.

His sense of things being "off," his sixth sense honed by years of bitter experience and narrowly won survival, warned him of what was to come about half a second before the tribespeople sprang their trap.

Dante flung himself toward a light post as half a dozen warriors emerged from the shadows simultaneously. His reflexes saved him—a crossbow bolt or perhaps a large dart whisked through the air where his head had been an instant before. The rest had only hand weapons, and with one terrible voice, they shouted as they converged on him.

"Stupid," he chided himself. At least his brain was still working in overdrive. He shouldn't have rushed in so blindly. It wasn't over yet, either.

The Dirtwalkers had slightly misjudged the angle of his approach, and he was already slipping out of the noose. They wouldn't be able to surround him in time to strike him down. He had a second or two to ruin their ambush, separate them from each other, and deal with the bastards one or two at a time. Fighting all six at once would be suicide, even for Dante.

He rolled laterally around the pole's base. The motion took him out of the swing range of the first raider. It was a husky, feral woman armed with a sickle-like sword. The blade struck the lamppost instead of Dante, chipping its edge as it deflected.

Dante responded with a fast repositioning of his feet and a gouging thrust at the woman's unprotected midsection. He felt the machete blade slice through flesh, and the woman gurgled horribly and slumped over.

Two more of her companions circled the light from the sides in a basic flanking maneuver. Rather than pivoting toward the closer of the two, Dante simply twisted his hands so the spear spun toward the man, flat edge facing him, and smacked him in the face. The blow halted his momentum. Dante slipped beyond him, moving backward toward the facility's abandoned courtyard as the others bounded after him.

Then someone burst out of a stand of withered bushes and seized Dante around the shoulders. The Marauder dropped his spear and instantly stabbed down, back, and up with the short sword, striking between his legs. The blade stuck in something relatively soft, probably the attacker's thigh muscle. Dante left it there and explosively dashed forward to slip out of the man's grasp.

Before he could retrieve his spear, the ambusher's fist lashed out and caught him in the side of the head. Dante reeled into a half-wall, crashed hard, and couldn't recover in time. The snarling raiders rose like a wave and blocked him off from every direction, about to engulf him.

He drew his knife. Three struck at once, and there was no way to dodge or block them all. A spearpoint lacerated his chest. The heavy material of his coat weakened the blow somewhat, but it still drew a hot, stinging line across his pectoral toward his armpit. Despite the pain that shot down through his arm, he grabbed the spear below the blade and yanked on it hard, pulling the wielder off-balance.

The others weren't idle. Three more of them were poised to finish him off with their raised axes and swords. In the back of his mind, Dante carried the grim satisfaction of knowing he'd taken several people with him into the afterlife. They'd not had an *easy* time killing him.

Then a chorus of blood-curdling shrieks rose from the adjacent shadows. Silhouettes jumped up toting weapons and pounced on the attackers before they could react. In a flash of dim light, Dante saw a face with crescent scars on her cheeks.

As the raiders reacted in shock and tried to adjust to the Harij's counter-ambush, Dante knocked aside a sword driving toward his heart and piled into its wielder. A brutal knife slash opened the man's throat as he tripped him and pushed him down.

Then a crush of bodies was against him, and it felt like something jabbed him in the leg. He could only strike blindly with his blade and razorfist until the human forms abruptly receded. He struggled to focus and saw the last attackers fleeing in desperate terror as the Harij drove them off.

A stillness set in, a firm understanding that it was over, although the chase was still on and people around him gasped and moaned. He forced himself to breathe and put away his weapons. His head swam from the thick smell of sweat and blood.

Dante took one step toward the tallest warrior who looked the most familiar. "Urshielle. Thank you. I..."

Then his body gave out. His legs stopped working, and his mind did nothing to correct them. He slumped to his knees and toppled onto his back on the ground. His vision went dark despite his eyes staying open.

Consciousness came and went, flitting and inconstant. The one thing he could say for certain—it had settled in his brain with the firmness of fact before he passed out—was that four or five sets of strong hands gripped him and bore him up. They carried him somewhere...perhaps, at last, to safety.

CHAPTER TEN

Nasreen

"Nasreen Joelle," Nasreen said while looking in the mirror. "Right now, at this moment, I get to be Nasreen Joelle." She paused, leaving her makeup only half applied. She breathed in through her nose and watched her nostrils dilate, then out through her mouth, which briefly left a foggy white spot on the shiny surface before her.

Her usual self, her "real" self, wasn't too hard on the eyes, and it was nice to see the woman she was only allowed to be in her free time. Soon, she would go to work once again, which meant temporarily being someone else.

Her hair was still its natural color, a deep golden honey shade that straddled the line between blonde and light brown. She would apply Quick-Dye as part of her disguise in a moment, and she had yet to decide what would be best. Platinum blonde, black, auburn, or something "unnatural" like blue, green, or pink were all on the table as long as she could style it differently from how she usually wore it, which was long, loose, and flowing, unbound.

Her eyes were the color of polished mahogany, a brown that

drew attention to what a lovely shade it was. They were nearly a copper-orange in the right light. Some people found it odd or intimidating, but mostly they thought it was beautiful.

She had changeable contacts, of course. Those, too, would be part of her ensemble once she assumed her next identity. She would decide on which hue her eyes would be once she'd selected a hair color.

Her jaw was a little broader than she'd like, but no one had ever called her unattractive so she'd not had it surgically altered. Otherwise, her face was as good as anyone could hope for. Symmetrical and proportionate, classically beautiful without being ostentatious. With the right makeup and a few other minor alterations, she could make her nose or cheekbones appear differently than they did in their default state. Her lips were the right degree of fullness to appear fuller or thinner as needed.

Her body had also chosen to cooperate with her chosen profession before her birth. Nasreen had always felt that she was quite literally born for the job.

She stood at a medium height for a woman. In flat shoes and with the right demeanor and mannerisms, she could seem smaller, timid, and petite. With platforms or heels and an opposite way of carrying herself, she could appear tall and domineering, commanding attention—especially from men—in either case. She was trim but not skinny since she kept herself fit enough that muscles filled out her limbs and accentuated her curves. She could also adjust her body shape with proper clothing choices, subtle undergarment accouterments, and simply by *thinking* of herself as bigger or smaller than she was by default.

"Yes," she said to the mirror. "It's good to be Nasreen. But not tonight. What is the name again?" She remembered it, but asking herself was part of the transformation ritual. "Ah, yes. Kara Hengst. That's who I'll be."

According to the concocted backstory, the supposed Ms.

Hengst was a pilot for hire from the Berlin Station, but she'd been operating low-key in Londonburg for a year in between gigs for still other Stations. She was a woman with some roots in her homeland but worldly enough that no one would be too bewildered by her way of speaking. A touch of a German accent still existed in an otherwise neutral, generic register that one would expect from someone who'd made their living hopping from city to city across the space-bound net that encircled the Earth.

Nasreen nodded and went back to applying her makeup, putting on the finishing touches. She used subtle shading tricks to make her nose appear ever so slightly broader and her cheeks narrower and more concave. She also emphasized the upturned corners of her eyes more than she normally would as Nasreen.

While she worked, she told herself in a quiet internal voice that this was how she'd *always* done her makeup because that was the way Kara Hengst had always done it, the best to emphasize her unique features.

Along similar lines, she quizzed herself on how Kara, the complete and real woman she'd created, would respond to the situation she was about to find herself in. What would be her starting attitude and how would she approach the people she needed to speak to? How would she deal with setbacks, and how would she celebrate small victories? What sorts of things would she bring up while making small talk?

How had Kara Hengst always behaved in situations like the one to come? After all, she'd been doing this stuff for years.

Nasreen decided that Kara, unlike herself, was a woman who occasionally showed vulnerability when it might have been better to show strength and remain cool and unflappable. By allowing hints of weakness to slip out, Kara would catch the attention of the sharks, the predators. Nasreen would take note of it. She would know who to watch out for.

She finished her makeup, admiring herself. Still beautiful, but...different. Exactly what she required.

There weren't many people out there who knew who Nasreen Joelle was. She was too good at her job for that. There was a small handful. Those who made it their business to recognize spies and infiltrators, hunt them down, and expose them, often assumed that a person like Nasreen would try to make herself look as *dissimilar* to her usual self as possible when going undercover.

To confound them, she selected the bottle of Quick-Dye labeled "platinum." Rather than go with a darker shade or something unusual, she would simply become a lighter shade of blonde.

After wrapping the towel around her face and neck, she sprayed the bottle's contents all through her long locks and combed it to ensure an even spread. Human hair tended to absorb the substances used in Quick-Dye almost instantly. The product then created a sort of leaching effect that meant it wasn't necessary to touch every single spot with the dye. It was one of the more convenient developments in cosmetic fashion technology of recent years.

It took about three to five minutes for the dye to completely set in and dry. Nasreen left the towel on for seven to be safe. During that time, she examined different outfits she'd laid out earlier. Three ensembles stretched across her bed in the adjacent room. She was already leaning toward the black one with the tight trousers and smoothed-out jacket. The maroon one with looser pants and a tighter top might also be an option.

"Black," she decided. "It will contrast nicely with the hair. And the eyes." Her contact lenses were disinfecting. She returned to the bathroom, took off the face towel, and removed them from the liquid. She rinsed them and inserted them, double-checking to ensure the lenses were correct since she had slight astigmatism.

Then she pulled out her sphere and found the program that

came with the lenses, setting it to a vibrant blue-green. Her vision went blurry for a second or two as they refocused and the chosen color articulated itself. When it finished, she spent a moment admiring her new "ice princess" look, then went back into the bedroom to change into the black outfit.

The final effect was of a woman who was "cute" enough that most men would take an interest in her while also underestimating her, yet not to the point that they wouldn't believe she was an accomplished pilot. As for other women, she didn't look *excessively* pretty, and she had no intention of acting flirtatiously enough to be annoying and arouse jealousy. That would be counterproductive.

Completing the job was the important thing. Nasreen continued to attract clients who wanted her unique services precisely because she could deliver the goods without personal issues getting in the way. Yet she'd always enjoyed the work. It filled a need within her for adventure—danger, even. Her parents had tried to keep her away from it, but she'd eagerly run toward it at every opportunity since her late teens.

The next things she needed to do before she set out for the evening were to practice her accent and mannerisms and review the case's facts. She decided to do both at once by reading off the dossier in her affected Kara Hengst voice. In front of the mirror, of course, to observe her hand movements, facial tics, and the like.

As she took up position and pulled the dossier into the air via her sphere's projector, something strange occurred to her.

She could no longer remember exactly what Nasreen Joelle had originally sounded like or what Nasreen Joelle's mannerisms had been. The other people she'd been over the years had nearly crowded Nasreen out of the picture.

For some reason, a shiver went through her. She rolled her shoulders and shook her head to dismiss it. "No, that's ridiculous," she muttered. "It doesn't matter. What's important is that

I'm in control at all times. The façades simply come with the territory."

As she prepared to read from the info sheet, mentally shifting into the persona of Ms. Hengst, the disturbing notions refused to go away.

She'd subconsciously thought of various other personae and how she could use those to reinforce the current one. Kara Hengst could refer to things that Mavis Tranh had seen, or Lia Ramirez had done. Her various false identities, her myriad cover stories, were so numerous, so deep and complex, that they might as well exist as firmly in truth as they did in pretense.

If Nasreen so desired, she could simply let Nasreen fade from the world altogether and slip into one of her other lives permanently. It wouldn't be hard.

"Stop it," she chided herself. She drew a deep breath, adjusted her new brilliantly platinum hair, and turned her eyes and concentration to the dossier.

As she read aloud, she let her voice slip into the completely neutral register she used as her generic "template" for a Station-hopper. Then she slowly incorporated slight vestiges of German pronunciation and diction where they felt natural and wouldn't be too hard to remember. She'd already practiced it a bit before, but it was good to refresh.

It was the same with the facts of the case. She remembered most of them, but it would be better to have every detail as fresh in her mind as possible.

Her client was the angry and grieving lover of a crew member who'd died on a Dirtside mission with a particular gang of Raiders. He hadn't known that his boyfriend was participating in such a dangerous expedition and the news of the other man's death came as a shock.

Furious and hungry for answers and suspicious of shady goings-on, he'd spread the word through the proper underground channels that he was in the market for someone who did freelance intelligence and espionage work.

Nasreen had heard and responded. Once the man had made it clear that he was willing and able to pay her fee, and once she'd assured herself that he seemed relatively trustworthy, she'd taken the job without too much coaxing. Boredom was looming overhead when she'd gone for their mutual interview. Life had been unacceptably quiet for weeks.

It had proven to be a complex job, though. Nasreen had been on it for over a month, and tonight would be the first time she met the crew. She'd had to deal with certain other things first.

Removing their usual pilot was the priority. If the man had proven clean, she could've arranged for him to have a minor injury that would've made him unable to fly or found some way to get him tied up with bullshit external affairs right when the crew needed him.

Fortunately for her, it had turned out that he was dealing various sorts of contraband on the side. Once Nasreen had discovered his criminal activities, it was a simple matter of anonymously exposing them to the authorities. With him locked up, there was no danger of him showing up to fly again at the last minute.

Of course, it meant that the Raiders' captain was in the market for a new shuttle pilot. Nasreen made sure that she—or Kara, rather—was the first to respond. Among her various skills, she was talented at bypassing security systems and hacking into pertinent databases. That allowed her to scrub dirt away from her reputation and that of her many aliases while simultaneously gathering dirt on her targets.

Unless she was gravely mistaken, the crew she'd be infiltrating was pretty fucking dirty. There was no way to prove anything yet, but there were far too many questions that lacked anything resembling good answers. There were many blank spots that could easily be full of nasty things, especially when a crewman had died in such a careless and unnecessary fashion.

As their new shuttle pilot, Nasreen's task would be simply to serve as a walking ear. Her client didn't want her to *do* much. She simply had to collect information passively. That cut down on the danger a great deal. Yet, she suspected there would still be a lot of risks involved with such a gang of pirates.

Kara Hengst would be the type who was tough and canny enough to ride with them while also being stupid. She was also naïve enough that they wouldn't suspect her of listening too closely to what was said or putting two and two together.

Nasreen finished reading the dossier in Kara's voice. While doing so she'd checked her mannerisms, lodging them in her brain to make habits out of them. She was satisfied that she had the role down pat.

She gathered up her things and made ready to leave the apartment. The meeting with her new crew would be at a dive bar on the Underside. Nasreen knew the neighborhood, but it would still take time to get there. She wanted to leave herself enough of a margin of error in case anything went wrong.

Before she opened the door to depart, she stopped in front of it, staring at its flat surface.

"Why are you doing this?" Her voice—Kara's voice, although Nasreen's was still audible within it—bounced back at her from its surface. "You have the talents to make an easier living. You can have any life you want, girl. Why do you keep putting yourself into situations where one slip-up means getting killed?"

She didn't have an easy answer to the question. Part of it, perversely enough, was self-explanatory. There was far less satisfaction in jobs that *didn't* involve the threat of death.

Besides, it kept her from getting too complacent. She didn't have to settle upon one life as most people did. She could sip from dozens of different lives, sample them all and switch between them at will, and get paid handsomely for doing so. In a way, life couldn't possibly have been better.

Even if she kept forgetting exactly who "Nasreen" was.

Once again shaking her head to banish pointless thoughts, Nasreen went through the door and out into the evening. If all went well, she might arrive at her ultimate destination within the next day or less.

The Northeastern American Sunken Sprawl. The ruins of a once-great city on the island of Atlantica, which had given its name to all the Stations in general. Kara had never been there before. Few people had.

She smiled as she stepped out of the building and into the freshly pumped air. There was a first time for everything.

CHAPTER ELEVEN

Dante

Dante somehow became aware that he lay beneath a flickering electrical light before he opened his eyes. Something about the dim red illumination it cast through his eyelids and a faint memory of primitive lights from when he was a child registered in his mind as his body remained half-dormant and slow to recover.

He was lying in a bed or something close enough to a bed. It was surprisingly comfortable, in any event. Not what he'd expected. A faint humming sound surrounded him, ambient and sourceless. It was probably the electricity used to power the over-head lights pulsing through hidden wires all around him.

Steeling himself for whatever revelations might await, Dante opened his eyes and took in the sight of his new environment.

As he'd been nearly positive was the case, he was indoors. Specifically in a dingy room on the smaller side but not quite cramped. It had a strange quality of being comfortable and anti-septic, old and worn-down, yet showing the signs of extensive human use and care. The air was thick. He couldn't tell if the room was above ground or below the surface.

His gaze turned down. He was lying on a hospital bed or something that closely approximated one. Like the rest of the room, it was old and worn, but someone had made a legitimate effort to keep it as clean as realistically expected. Wiggling his hands and feet, he determined that he was naked but covered by a sheet to his chest.

Off to the side in the corner were his clothes and all of his gear and equipment, everything he'd had when he collapsed. It looked as though his clothes had received a cursory cleaning. Unless he was mistaken, none of his valuables were missing. Whoever had put him here was simply storing his things and getting them out of the way for the moment.

It was puzzling. Theft, whether from the living or the dead, was a way of life on Earth. He wondered if he was still on the planet. Someone might have rescued him, and he was now on a ship or perhaps one of the more peripheral backwater Stations.

Space and the Stations had a different *feel* than Earth did, though. A different smell. An indescribable quality of the air. Impossible though it would seem, he must still be Dirtside.

He was right about the light. It was an old-fashioned fluorescent tube flickering in a highly annoying fashion.

"Fuck me," he muttered in a low, breathy gasp. The pain of his wounds was coming back to haunt him. He'd almost forgotten about the spear cut along his chest and the potential jab he'd taken to the leg.

He pulled the sheet away from his torso and looked down at himself, raising his hands to prod things if necessary and trace along. Bandages encircled his upper torso and shoulder. They were clean and applied by someone who knew what they were doing. He also suspected, based on the nature of the dull but growing pain, that whoever tended him had stitched the wound.

Dante ran his hand down his leg next. He hadn't been quite sure if he'd truly taken an injury. By the time it had occurred to him that he might be hurt again, his mind and body were already on the verge of giving out. His perceptions had been distorted by his other pains, plus the cocktail of adrenaline, fatigue, and stimulants.

He found another bandaged patch, smaller this time. The pain was sharper when he pressed on it but contained within a narrower area. That meant a knife or spearpoint had probably stabbed him. Not deep enough to completely disable the leg, but enough to make his life more difficult than it needed to be for a while.

"Well," he murmured. "At least whoever patched me up wasn't an amateur." Although no master surgeon, he'd acquired substantial experience as a respectable field medic. Enough to know that his rescuer had done a good job.

Probably better than he could've done himself with the right equipment. Dante always had plenty of medical supplies on the ship. He'd insisted on it. Dermal seals and stimpacks weren't always enough should he ever find himself badly hurt and stranded on Earth.

He laid back and tried to relax. Two things happened that were totally out of character and sent a creeping chill down his spine.

The phrase "stranded on Earth" seemed to echo in his mind. Somewhere outside, he heard the wind. There was no wind in space or on the Stations. He was Dirtside without a ship. The ruined planet was now holding him prisoner.

He had to get out of here. Legendary as his survival stories had become, the Earth was not his home, and being trapped on it was one of the few things he regarded as a nightmare scenario. It had occurred to him the evening before, he recalled, after he'd watched his ship and Hyde's rise into the sky without him. He'd been so keyed up on desperation and bloodlust that the situation's true horror hadn't impressed itself until now.

There was always a way. Other ships came down to the planet all the time, really. He simply needed to survive long enough to hitch a ride. A *friendly* ride if possible, but he wasn't above hijacking one at knifepoint if that was what it took.

Then footsteps approached, heavy yet somehow gentle. The door opened, interrupting his ruminations. He tensed, and his alertness went back to maximum. There was nothing to suggest that anyone here meant him harm—they were trying to nurse him back to health, after all—but he refused to get too comfortable or complacent until he knew exactly what the hell was going on.

The figure who came through the door was tall but bent and carried a battered metal tray with various things on it. Though completely bald, Dante briefly wondered if they were a man or a woman. He settled on man after a moment but retained a certain curiosity if the person might have a hormonal anomaly or something. There was another possibility, but he didn't bother to entertain it.

"Good day," the bald man greeted him in a low, soothing voice. He spoke the Dirtwalker trade tongue with an accent not too dissimilar from the tall spear woman Dante had met on the roof. "I hope you're well. If you feel up to it, I wish to check your wounds and replace the dressing. How do you feel, friend?"

Dante slowly raised himself to something that resembled a sitting posture, but he had to be careful to avoid putting unnecessary strain on his chest, back, or leg. "I'm not too bad. All things considered. Are you the one who patched me up?"

"Yes." The man set the tray down on a small, crude table. On it were fresh bandages, a pair of scissors, and a bowl filled with a liquid that steamed gently and gave off a slight chemical disinfectant odor. "My name is Raphorien. What is yours?"

Dante started to relax. This man must have been a designated healer, and there was no reason to suspect that anything was amiss. Anyone who'd wanted him dead would've had ample opportunities to do the deed while he lay passed out.

"Dante Shale. Good to meet you, Raphorien."

He examined his caretaker in more detail. Raphorien was, paradoxically for such a large man, incredibly harmless-looking. He had soft facial features that seemed permanently set in a mild expression of kindness and concern, and his body was also soft and unthreatening. His big hands worked with a kind of mincing precision.

Circling his bald head above the brow was a ring of sickle-shaped scars. Although smaller and more numerous, the basic design was the same as what Dante had earlier seen on the face of the warrior woman who'd held him at spearpoint. For some reason, he was having trouble remembering her name.

Raphorien pulled up a chair beside the bed, the scissors in his hand. Dante noted that they were small with blunted tips, as though the healer had chosen them specifically to look as non-threatening as possible. "I will now cut off the old bandages if you permit it."

"First, tell me where I am and everything that's happened since I arrived here. How long have I been out?"

The physician offered a small smile as a gesture of conciliation. He then explained things with a patient straightforwardness not unlike how an adult would speak to a child, but it didn't seem condescending. It was simply an extension of the man's caring and paternal nature.

"Very well. You are within the commune of the Crescent-Marked. Urshielle brought you here after the battle with the Demorquen tribe. You were exhausted, and when you spoke, you spoke only the nonsense of dreams. We treated your wounds and let you rest.

"It has been about a day and a half since you arrived. It was past dark when you came here, then there was a full day, and now it is morning again. You roused long enough for us to give you food and water, although you were not yourself and you might not remember it."

Dante nodded. He had no memory of waking up or drinking and eating anything, but it made sense. He didn't feel as hungry or thirsty as expected after around thirty-six hours.

He was about to ask more, but Raphorien added, "You are not being held here as a prisoner. We are caring for you to show our thanks for your aid to the Harij. If you so desire, you may leave at any time. I'm afraid I would not recommend it. You still have much recovering to do before your body serves you as well as it could."

"Yeah," the Marauder agreed. "You're right about that. You can change the bandages now. Tell me, though, what exactly is this place? What's the significance of the 'Crescent-Marked?' I've spent a lot of time Dirtside—on Earth, I mean—but it's something I've never seen or heard of before. This is my first time on Old Atlantica."

Raphorien leaned forward, slipped the blunted tip of the lower scissor blade beneath the dressing on Dante's chest wound, and carefully cut it away while avoiding the injury itself as much as possible. He was trying not to cause any pain to his patient unless strictly necessary.

"Ah, I see," the healer replied. "We, the Crescent-Marked, are a...a group, a tribe without a tribe. I do not know what the word would be in your language. We serve a sacred function that is respected by most other tribes, although some have breached the peace agreement. We have warriors who the others may kill if they participate in open feuds, as Urshielle chose to do on behalf of the Harij. None may assail our sanctuary without incurring the anger of the other tribes."

It made sense. They were something like a monastic order, then. That implied certain other things about them. The symbol of the crescent was beginning to make sense. Dirtwalker mythology held that people like Dante and other off-planet Plunderers came from the moon.

Raphorien went on, "Our members come from those who have been moon-scraped or moon-plucked. After such a fate, we are no longer suitable for the normal roles among our people's tribes so we come here to practice our arts."

The final piece of the puzzle fell into place as Dante's memory yielded information he'd nearly forgotten about. "Moon-scraped" was a Dirtwalker term for women who'd been subject to o-harvesting. "Moon-plucked" meant something similar—namely, t-harvesting.

The Raiders didn't do it as often as its counterpart procedure. Only pubescent boys were candidates for testicle removal to collect the large amounts of reproductive hormones found within them. Once it had been as common as o-harvesting, but in more recent times the Stations had made vast improvements to synthesizing artificial testosterone. Still, it wasn't unheard of.

Thus, as the female Crescent-Marked were barren women, Raphorien was a eunuch.

Dante wasn't the sentimental type. But as the healer worked on him with compassion he probably didn't deserve, it was difficult not to feel a faint pang in his stomach, a slight tightening of his throat, for the tragedy of these people's existence.

Raphorien continued, "We call our women the Crescent-Kissed, or simply the Kissed. They train as warriors to defend our home against those who would break the accords, and to act as mediators in the conflicts of others when the violence threatens to become too widespread."

That more or less answered another question Dante had been reflecting upon. The woman with the spear—her name was

Urshielle, he recalled—hadn't been a Harij, although she might have been a *former* member of said tribe. Instead, she'd come to offer aid after the Reapers had destroyed most of them and conducted their o-harvest.

"Our men we call the Crescent-Crowned, or simply the Crowned. We train to become healers, studying the ancient arts left over from the Old World. We cannot restore all the secrets of medicine from those times. They require tools and magic we do not possess. Much of it is still understandable, and we have honed our craft until if it is within our power, all who come to us for healing will leave better than they were when they arrived."

By this point, Raphorien had removed the dressing on the chest wound and was dabbing it with a cloth soaked in the steaming antiseptic liquid. It stung, but not as badly as Dante had feared. He gritted his teeth and bore it. Better a few moments of pain now than a debilitating infection later.

Next, he had Dante roll onto his side so he could change the dressing on the gunshot wound. Dante had almost forgotten about that one.

To distract himself, Dante inquired, "Why do you use the crescent symbol?" He had at least one suspicion, but it would be better to hear the healer say the truth outright rather than put too much faith in his assumptions.

Raphorien mopped the excess liquid up with a dry rag, then began preparing the fresh bandages. "Because it reminds us of the Moonfiends, of course. Also because the scars left by moon-scraping and moon-plucking look much like crescents themselves."

The first reason was exactly what Dante had expected, but strangely enough, the second hadn't occurred to him. An image flashed in his mind of the crowd of Harij women on the roof behind Urshielle, all bearing the gyno-extractor scars on their lower torsos. They *did* look somewhat like a crescent moon.

"I understand that you are of the Moonfolk yourself, although it seems you are different from the worst of them. Seeing you up close confirms what many of us had long thought, which is that you are people like us in most ways. Some believe you are a different thing entirely, like the Nightmutts, but in the shape of men. Others of us have long held that you are humans who fled from Earth during the dark times."

Dante lifted his arm to allow the physician better access to his laceration. "Yes. That's what we are. I'm surprised to learn about you, the Crescent-Marked, though. I thought all the tribes hated each other too much for people from different ones to work together so closely."

Raphorien shrugged. "We are not considered part of our birth tribes anymore. Those who survived the stealing of our fertility were often abandoned to the wastes or killed outright if we did not flee in shame. They think we are cursed or have become useless to our people. With the arts we have taught ourselves, we have attained a measure of respect from those who cast us out. And so there is new life for those of us willing to learn."

Dante was silent for a moment while the healer worked. He'd never heard about the commune before, nor would such a thing have occurred to him. He'd learned more about the Dirtwalkers than most people of the Atlantican Stations, but he still thought of them primarily as hazards to be avoided, managed, or destroyed. Their private lives and the bonds between them in the daily struggle for survival weren't things he'd reflected much upon.

"I suppose we all do what we must to get by," he murmured.

Raphorien finished dressing the chest wound and moved to Dante's leg. He repeated the process, which went more quickly since the stab covered a smaller area. When he was close to finished, the physician said, "I will bring you food and water soon. Lie back for now. After you eat, it might be best for you to sleep again. We will keep a close eye on you if you wish it."

Dante felt stronger and livelier than he would've expected. Instead of leaning back on the battered old pillow beneath his head, though, he reached out and caught the edge of the healer's frayed robe. "The woman who saved me. Urshielle, that was her name, wasn't it? I need to speak to her."

Raphorien looked at him with a mild expression of surprise, or at least some emotion that suggested he took the request seriously. "Oh, yes. I can have her see you, but not right now. I am afraid she is currently engaged with something. You may speak to her soon. For now, you must rest, for your own sake."

"Very well." The Marauder made a show of leaning back against the pillow and letting the tension drain from his body as he unfocused his eyes, allowing the lids to droop. "Thank you, Raphorien."

The large, gentle-featured man gave him a brief bow of his shiny head. "Of course, of course. All things will heal in time."

Dante waited for him to leave. He listened carefully to the slow, heavy, shuffling footsteps of the Crowned man, counting them and judging their distance, then adding a margin of safety.

Minutes passed, and he grew confident that not only was Raphorien gone, but no one else was nearby or on their way into the makeshift hospital room.

"Good," he whispered. Then he threw off the sheet and rolled out of bed.

He favored his leg but still got a mild jab of pain from the wounds on his chest and back and the stab in his thigh. Fortunately, no red stain appeared through the fresh bandages.

Once he'd adjusted himself and had a better feel for his current physical capabilities, he went over to the pile of his things in the corner. Using caution but trying to waste as little time as possible, he dressed in his underclothes, trousers, shirt, and boots. Then, inhaling deeply, he found his sheathed knife and added it to his belt. His razorfist was there too, but wearing such a weapon in a place that had shown him nothing but hospitality so far would seem suspicious. Knives were useful everyday tools as well as weapons. Everyone carried them.

Stiffness and tenderness inhibited his movements, but Dante had been injured enough times in the past that he knew how to work around such things and make the most of his body's limited functionality. He quickly reset his gait into a fast, smooth shuffle. It wasn't as quick or graceful as his usual stride, but it would do.

He was pretty sure he trusted Raphorien. Perhaps even Urshielle. Still, it was totally against his nature to lie passively in bed and hope that other people would shower him with goodwill. He intended to assess the situation, come what may.

Dante opened the door. It wasn't locked, which made sense. Raphorien had said he could leave whenever he wanted. Unless he grossly misunderstood what the man had meant, he was doing nothing wrong by taking a stroll through the place.

Beyond the door lay a hallway lined with other entries, which likely led to rooms similar to his. The stark design and faded posters marked the building as undeniably an old, repurposed hospital. Dante wondered if the commune was based entirely within it or if the Crescent-Marked had an entire complex of structures like the Harij.

Lights flickered, making the place less desolate than it might have looked otherwise. Only about one fixture per hallway worked. They might have deliberately disconnected the extraneous ones to save on their limited electricity supply.

Dante casually strolled down the longest corridor he could find. He kept his steps quiet and movements unobtrusive but otherwise made no particular effort to hide. The feel of the place reinforced what the healer had told him. There was no reason to assume that angry guards would tackle him for daring to emerge from his room.

Then again, if Urshielle were representative of their women, he would prefer not to take unnecessary risks in angering them.

Some of the doors he passed hung open, and within the

chambers beyond them were other wounded people languishing in beds and being tended to by Moon-Crowned men. The other healers had a general look about them similar to Raphorien's. It must have been the result of having their physical development interfered with by t-harvesting.

No one seemed to notice him. If they did, they didn't care that he was up and about.

Towards the end of the long hallway, Dante saw something that caught his interest. A long glass surface, a window, with natural light streaming through it. It contained a door that opened out.

He guessed at first that he must be on the hospital's ground floor and it was an exit or entrance. When he drew closer, he saw that it opened onto a balcony overlooking a small courtyard surrounded by different wings of the building.

He was on the second floor. On the ground beneath the balcony was a group of people—five women, from the look of it. Curious, Dante opened the glass door and wandered partway out toward the railing.

The courtyard contained a crude fountain, a living tree, and several small bushes or potted plants. They looked sickly, but at least the Crescent-Marked had managed to keep them alive. Any form of agriculture or horticulture on Earth had become far more difficult since the core had begun its slow death spiral.

Then, blinking, Dante felt his heart leap up to pound against his ribs. One of the five women knelt on the ground, restrained by three others. Two women flanked her and held her arms. The third stood behind her, bracing the girl's head against her body with both hands. The fifth was Urshielle. A knife was in her hand.

The tall warrior advanced. The blade flashed under the dim brownish sunlight with its point aimed straight for the girl's face. She trembled and whimpered in terror, and tears rolled down her cheeks.

Dante suddenly felt like he was choking. For all the violence he'd witnessed in his time, something about the young woman's pitiful state and the cruelty he knew would come struck him low in the gut, leaving him sickened.

"No," he gasped and spun. There had to be a way down. There had to be time to stop it.

CHAPTER TWELVE

Nasreen

"Kara Hengst," Nasreen said to herself, examining her face—a new face, yet so strangely familiar—in the reflected portal created by her sphere's camera. "My name is Kara Hengst." She smiled, consciously twisting her lips in a way that differed slightly from her usual, natural smile.

She was in the bathroom on one of the shuttle trains that went to Lower Londonburg, also known as the Underside or simply the Unders. She had a couple of minutes before they arrived at their destination and wanted privacy to practice her introduction one last time. If anyone overheard, it wasn't a problem. A person practicing for a job interview wasn't strange or uncommon. Although most people used their real names and faces.

Satisfied, she dismissed the camera and collapsed the sphere before returning it to her pocket. When she stepped out of the bathroom, a man eyed her in irritation for having taken so long. There was a momentary flash of interest as his gaze moved over her face and body, but his other business was more pressing. He rushed in after her and slammed the door.

Nasreen walked out and found her seat again, glad that no one had taken it, although there was still standing space. Recent advances in shuttle gravitech meant the ride was astoundingly smooth so passengers could walk to and fro on the vehicle without potentially losing their balance or getting motion sickness.

She made herself comfortable. Then waited.

It didn't take long. The synthesized voice of the shuttle train's AI announced that their stop in Lower Londonburg was coming up.

Unlike most other major city sectors, the Unders had only a single stop on most public transportation routes. It was near the main business district of that part of town, with a couple of government buildings nearby. The dingy, foreboding aspect of the place was still quite noticeable. For casual visitors, it kept them within areas where they weren't too likely to end up bleeding in an alley if anyone found them again at all.

Nasreen's business would take her considerably beyond this pale circle of relative safety. Lower Londonburg had a lot of places the average person didn't know about and were all the better for it.

It was one of the oldest parts of the city. Much of it dated from the station's early construction, little more than a foundation on which to build the rest. It had grown its own housing complexes, bodegas, and holes-in-the-wall, regardless. The people who lived or lounged there were generally among the city's poorest denizens, the unfortunate castoffs, the new arrivals struggling to work their way up, and the like. Things were cheaper there—including life.

It also hosted popular gathering places for ne'er-do-wells and the less reputable sorts of Plunderers and Raiders. Polite society generally didn't bother to look too closely at anything going on

Underside. One could find a measure of privacy there, provided one knew how to filter out the squealers who might reveal their affairs to the authorities or their rivals.

The shuttle train came to a nice smooth halt, and Nasreen rose from her seat, sliding out into the aisle and departing without a word. Only one other person was getting off at the same stop, a grizzled older man. He was out in front of her, moving slower than she would've liked, but once he stepped out of the train, he immediately turned right and stumbled off into the shadows.

Nasreen went straight out from the platform. Reaching the bar would require her to cross the square and duck into a maze of relatively narrow lanes. Some were more like alleys than streets since they were formed simply of gaps between buildings or parts of the station's superstructure. Much of the Unders was like that—an informal jumble where people did things between the cracks, shielded from sight by the rest of the station that loomed above their heads.

The sun had drifted behind the Earth. The main Lower Londonburg Square was always flooded with cheap but effective lighting to put inexperienced visitors at ease and cut down on crime. Beyond it, much of the district was about as dark at night as if it were deep within a warehouse basement.

A few shifty-looking characters eyed Nasreen as she passed. She noted them but otherwise ignored them, and no one tried anything. She'd learned how to project a particular vibe that tended to scare off all but the most committed predators or the ones too addled by drugs or insanity to exercise good judgment.

Soon she came to the north side of the square where the ring of white light ended, and the gloom began. She knew the darkened areas well enough that it was no problem to select a street other than Thornberry. Thornberry was her usual, but tonight a group of people was huddled there, and she'd rather not find out what they were doing. She entered the next street down, Thistle, instead. From there, it was a simple matter to take a left and bear northwest toward one of the Underside's two major red-light districts.

The bar where her new crew would be meeting was called Jel's, presumably after the founder or proprietor. Nasreen wasn't specifically aware of anyone by that name who worked there. She'd checked the place's files and notes beforehand. It was a dive, not a place to take lightly, but not an outright murder pit. She figured she could handle herself fine. Particularly as the guest of a Raider outfit who seemed to be regulars.

She saw the crew before she saw the bar. The group was standing around in the street, talking loudly. They were hard to mistake for anything other than the pirates they were. It was only a second or so after Nasreen had marked them that she identified the building behind them, notably by the red holographic "J" on its front display. A massive pipe that ran up through the bottom of the station before providing some or another utility to the main city blocked the rest of it.

Nasreen approached with a soft step and a neutral demeanor. She didn't bother trying to hide. She simply didn't attract attention to herself until she'd had time to observe the group. They were about what she'd expected—rowdy, tough-looking, alternately sullen and viciously funny, judging by the sharp peals of laughter that rose from their midst.

There were ten or twelve of them. Enough to pull off the heists typical of a bottom-feeding outfit, but not enough to become unwieldy and overly expensive in terms of dividing up the spoils. Near the group's center was a figure who had to be their leader, Captain Reavo.

"Hey!" a high-pitched, grating voice called. It was Reavo, and she'd noticed the approaching Nasreen. Or, rather, the approaching Kara.

Nasreen raised a hand briefly to acknowledge her. As she got closer, the light shifted so she got a better look at the whole crew as they all turned to look at her.

Most of them were men, ranging in approximate age from twenty-five to fifty-five, and from every background imaginable. There was a heavyset older woman off to the side who seemed to be part of a couple with a similar-looking man. The only other female member was Reavo herself.

She was smaller than Nasreen expected. She was the smallest person in the group, nearly a full head shorter than Nasreen and skinny. Something about the way she carried herself indicated a tough, scrappy ferociousness, though. She'd probably learned to compensate for her small size early in life by savaging anyone who tried to talk down to her or take advantage of her. She had curly dark hair tied back under her hat, and she wore big padded gloves. At least one of them probably concealed a pseudo-razor-fist, Nasreen guessed.

For an instant, Nasreen wondered if she'd made a mistake in creating Kara Hengst the way she had. A bigger, tougher, more sophisticated woman might've been a better foil to Reavo. There were still plenty of opportunities to learn more about her marks before she invested too deeply.

"Hi," Nasreen greeted them. "I'm Kara Hengst, the pilot. You're Reavo's crew?" She thickened the German accent a bit more than she'd first intended.

Reavo stepped forward. She had a strutting, almost lunging way of moving. "Yeah. Come here. Let's get a look at you. Fuck's sake, you don't look like you belong here. You must usually work for those *respectable* crews or something."

The other crew members laughed in low voices. Nasreen ignored it. She'd expected a certain amount of hazing. Nonetheless, she could instantly tell that Reavo would be a tough nut to crack.

She scanned her brain for information on the captain. The woman's real name was Calliope Reeves. She had multiple criminal convictions, but mostly petty stuff from her youth. Her record as an adult almost seemed *too* clean, if anything. She'd named her shuttle after herself and seemed to command a certain begrudging respect from people who knew she existed.

Nasreen was suddenly in their midst. It was impossible to be entirely at ease, but being too cool would've aroused their suspicion anyway. They were the rough crowd that expected new meat to be a tad nervous.

Nasreen gestured at the building. "Let's go in. I would like a drink before we talk business."

"Oh, really?" some guy from the back of the crowd grunted.

Reavo smirked. "Yeah, sure, but we don't drink with people who aren't what they say they are. What can you fly?"

"What do you mean?" Nasreen asked. She tried to convey that the question didn't intimidate her, only that the language barrier made it hard for her to grasp whatever Reavo's unspoken assumptions were.

"I mean what types of ships have you flown before or trained on?" The smaller woman spoke in a cawing, irritated voice. "Pretty fucking obvious question to ask a pilot."

Nasreen let out a brief snorting chuckle. "Yes, it is. You didn't tell me what type of shuttle you have, but..." She listed half a dozen different models in the size range appropriate for a crew of about a dozen.

In fact, she *did* know what type of ship they flew—that had been an essential part of the homework, especially when tailing their former pilot—but she didn't let them know as much. She casually dropped the model's name into the middle of her list.

Reavo raised her hands and spread her gloved fingers in a sarcastically dramatic motion. "Oooh, so many! Okay, fine, you mentioned the HR-89. That's what we've got. The *Reavo*. Just because you can fly doesn't mean you're *good*. I've taken over for pilots who didn't know what the hell they were doing. Or ones who got themselves killed being idiots. Let's get a drink though. We'll go over the rest inside."

Within, the bar was nearly empty. The only other patron was a long-faced older man drinking quietly in the corner. Reavo's crew ignored him and occupied an entire wing along the far end. Nasreen noticed, with faint respect, that they positioned themselves where they could easily watch anyone coming in through the front entrance *or* from the back of the building.

Working the bar was a bald older man with tattoos covering his forearms and a tarty younger woman with tired eyes. They brought out beers, two pitchers along with pint mugs, and otherwise left the Raiders to do as they pleased.

Mostly they bullshitted with one another, but Reavo and a handful of other men focused most of their attention on Kara. The captain seemed to take the hiring process quite seriously. She had plenty of anecdotes to prove it.

"...and I don't give a shit *what* you heard from people like Sanderson or Dirtboy, if you do the job, we pay you. They've cheated more people for real than I ever thought about cheating. That's the thing, though."

Reavo thumped her chest. "If you *don't* do the fucking job, you're dead. Either because you get yourself that way being a fool or because you endanger all of us and we take you out for our good. Understand? If you can do the job, you're fine. But don't fucking expect us to get all charitable about holding the hand of someone who's goddamn incompetent."

Nasreen nodded, paying attention to how Reavo's three top henchmen watched her. "I understand completely. You don't think I would've come to a place like this—with you people, no less—if I didn't believe in my abilities, do you?"

She twisted her mouth at the end of the comment and let her eyes sparkle a little.

Reavo stared at her, but the big bearded guy over her shoulder cracked up laughing. "Ha! We finally got someone who thinks as highly of herself as the captain does. Don't see that very often."

"Shut the fuck up," Reavo snapped at him, but when she looked back at Nasreen, she dispelled the fit of anger in an instant, and her usual cruel overconfidence returned. "Yeah, I guess not. You ever been to Old Atlantica, though?"

Nasreen shrugged. "It cannot be any worse than the other dead cities on Earth. I have been Dirtside many times, and I still have both of my arms, legs, eyes, and everything else. Besides, I'm a pilot. I'll come with you onto the ground if I have to, but it's usually smarter for pilots to wait with the shuttle, is it not?"

A man who'd positioned himself at the edge of Reavo's inner circle spoke up. "Good point, Hengst. Good point." He was a lean, handsome man, probably no older than thirty. Nasreen had been trying to determine whether he was listening to the interview or paying more attention to his buddies' joking around. His comment clarified the matter at once.

Reavo snorted. "So goddamn charming, Grind. Not every bitch is that easily wooed, though." She looked back at Nasreen. "If we get you in the pilot's seat and like what you can do during liftoff, you'll get the first third of your money then. The rest comes after we do the job. And no, we don't compromise on that, so don't waste our time arguing that you deserve *half* or that you deserve it *right now* because you don't."

Rolling her shoulders, Nasreen quipped, "A third at the start of the mission is fair."

The rumors she'd collected indicated that while other Raiders somewhat respected Reavo's crew, they weren't particularly well-liked by former members—some of whom complained of being stiffed on their pay. One even said they'd assaulted and tried to kill him in an argument.

It made sense. Reavo's policy would allow her to pay people she liked to keep them on board. If she didn't like them or couldn't afford them, she could claim that she'd "had" to kill them or chase them off "for the crew's safety." She seemed to realize that anyone who wasn't a moron would see through it. That only contributed to her arrogance and hostility.

"Okay," Reavo grumbled. "Describe how to fly an HR-89 from the Unders dock to the Northeast Sprawl. Don't act like we're too stupid to understand the technical details. We know all that shit. Be a professional."

Nasreen smiled. The HR-89 was one of her two favorite models. She explained in detail every step of the procedure. Since she hadn't been to Old Atlantica, she had to admit slight ignorance of the details, but she could fill them in with her experiences on flights to other, similar locations. In some cases, flights to places far harder to reach. At least Londonburg was on the same side of the planet as the island.

After a few more veiled threats and unnecessary questions, where Reavo's abrasiveness kept flaring up for no particular reason—and which Nasreen parried with a mixture of innocence and sarcasm—the interview finally ended.

The captain looked at her chief minions, including the handsome one called Grind. "Okay, then, Hengst. You're hired. Don't disappoint us. Now, here are the details of the mission. The gist is, we're going into the Sprawl to collect some metals. Pretty basic shit, might involve going into the shafts, though. What we'll do is..."

Nasreen already knew most of what the woman told her, but she played along, nodding and making the occasional astute remark, much to the captain's annoyance. And Grind's amusement.

For all her professionalism, Nasreen found it hard not to be distracted by the man. Something about the wolfish look on his face combined with his improbably pristine beauty—he looked out of place amid the rest of them—reminded her of how little time she'd had lately for recreational activities.

The crew went over the boring but necessary negotiations of

how much they expected to make and how they'd divide the profits. Since Nasreen's main payday came not from Reavo but from her client, she wasn't overly concerned. If she could walk away from the spy job with a bonus, so much the better.

As the last of the business talks drew to a close and the third and fourth pitchers of beer dwindled to emptiness, most of the crew got up and excused themselves. They either planned to meet with other people—friends, family, prostitutes—or simply to get a long night's sleep. Reavo had scheduled them to depart late morning.

The last to remain were Nasreen, Reavo, and Grind.

"Okay," the captain said, "I'm going. Don't be late. That's a bad way to make a first impression, Hengst."

Nasreen smiled and watched her leave. Once the small woman was gone, Grind slid over next to her.

"Hi," he said.

She smirked at him, ratcheting up the charm level to match his. "No need to introduce yourself, Grind. We've been sitting here together for an hour already. I know your name."

He spread his hands and made a mock pouty face. "It seemed...appropriate. Being around those guys I feel like I have a responsibility to be a gentleman. Sometimes."

"Oh?" She cocked an eyebrow. "Why, do you think I'm a lady or something?"

He stretched his arms. "Not sure yet. Want to dance? That will help me figure it out."

"I *suppose* we can do that." She looked at the bartender. "Music, please."

The bald man seemed a bit annoyed by the request, but he obliged them, powering up the holo-speakers with some vapid, bouncy song that Nasreen had heard at a few of the clubs lately. It was stupid but fun, and as she rose to her feet, the movements came naturally. Particularly since she was a bit drunk.

Grind was a better dancer than she was. She'd figured he

would be. He moved circles around her, but in ways that didn't make her feel too badly outshined. She was starting to like him. His interest in her seemed relatively sincere.

A woman who lived so many different lives didn't have time to invest fully in any one of them. Exciting though it was, it could get lonely.

She laughed and pretended to half-fall toward the wall so Grind would catch her. He did. His hands were on the slender, even bony side, but he had a nice strong grip. Looking into his black, sparkling eyes, she suspected that she *might* be making a mistake.

Still, the first part of the job, the hardest part, had gone well. She felt lucky. Lucky enough to have some fun. She certainly trusted herself enough not to do anything *too* stupid.

CHAPTER THIRTEEN

Dante

Limping at the maximum speed he could with a stab wound in his leg, Dante burst through the glass door he'd left open, leaving the balcony behind and swinging back into the second-floor hallway. He looked left and right, frantically seeking a stairwell or elevator. Anything that could get him to the first floor to stop Urshielle from killing the poor captive girl.

He cursed himself for not looking for stairs earlier. Since he couldn't recall seeing any as he approached the balcony, he went in the opposite direction instead. The dull ache in his leg grew in intensity, warning him with pain to scale back his exertions, but he ignored it.

Past the glass window that overlooked the courtyard, he came to an alcove where one half of a double door was propped open. Beyond it were steps. Dante threw himself toward them.

He knew he was aggravating his injuries. He also knew that he probably wouldn't make it in time. Reaching the courtyard might take a full minute, and Urshielle's blade had been seconds from the girl's throat. It didn't matter, though. He had to try.

Negotiating the stairs was a nightmare writ large, compressed into the span of fifteen or twenty seconds that felt like an hour. Jogging down them by alternating from one foot to the other proved impossible almost immediately. His leg seized up and radiated waves of pain that nearly made him fall to the first landing.

Instead, he leaned against the wall and hopped down on his good leg, taking the steps two at a time and thankful that his chest and back wounds were on the opposite side from the shoulder impacting the wall. He repeated the process after crossing the landing, knowing he must look ridiculous to anyone who might be watching. It was a stupid thing to worry about, but it only added to the humiliating sense that he was about to rack up *another* failure. It had been many years since he'd had a week even half this bad.

At the bottom of the second flight, a door to the right opened into the courtyard. A young woman's voice moaned and whimpered. The sound rose to a shrill scream as he pushed open the door and stumbled out into the air beyond. The natural earth felt strange under his feet after his struggle on the steps.

Urshielle retracted the knife. She'd finished her work. Dante had been too late—but he'd also misjudged the situation. The girl still lived.

Two red crescents now stretched from the sides of her mouth to the corners of her eyes, sending streams of bright red blood down her cheeks to mingle with the half-dried tears. They'd marked her. The women were inducting her into the ranks of the Crescent-Kissed.

Dante stopped. His chest heaved, and his body trembled with pain as he leaned against one of the columns that supported the balcony he'd perched upon. Sweat covered him, and the cool air felt strangely good. Despite being enclosed on all sides, a breeze was somehow dipping into the courtyard from the sky above.

Two of the women holding the new girl glanced briefly at him and turned away, as though mildly irritated by the interruption but otherwise unconcerned. He also sensed that Urshielle knew he was there but chose to ignore him until the ceremony was complete.

"Sister," Urshielle began and placed a hand atop the smaller woman's head. "Do not flinch from the pain and blood, for they are nothing compared to what you have already suffered. The kiss of the knife is the same as the kiss that welcomes you into our ranks. The scars on your face mirror those on your body. The pain you feel is no less than what we have felt too, and between us, there shall always be that bond."

She leaned over and kissed the girl on both lacerated cheeks, the blood making her lips garishly bright on her otherwise unadorned face. Then she stepped aside.

Each of the other three warrior women repeated the words that their leader had said and likewise kissed their newest member's bleeding cheeks. The girl was beginning to recover, Dante saw. She was steeling herself and accepting what had happened.

He wondered to what extent she'd consented to the procedure. It seemed unlikely that they'd *forced* it upon her, exactly, yet what other options did she have? If she didn't agree to become one of the Crescent-Marked, she would've had to make her way alone in a hostile world where most of her tribe was already dead.

When the others had all said their piece, Urshielle returned to her position in front of the inductee, again placing her strong hand atop the woman's head. "Let us swear the oath of loyalty and allegiance. To one another, and to the cause of fighting the Moonfiends unto the last blow, those who have killed that which gives life from within us. To you, sister Majala, *I swear that oath.*"

Urshielle's trio of assistants chimed in next, adding, "And I!"

Majala, the freshly scarred girl, looked like a different person than she had mere minutes ago. The fear and pain were gone, replaced by a somber dignity and fierce determination. "To you, my new sisters," she replied, in a voice barely above a whisper yet hardly weak, "I swear that oath."

Urshielle took her hand from the inductee's head. "Rise now, Majala, as one of the Crescent-Kissed."

She did, slowly. Although not a large woman, it seemed she stood taller and prouder than her natural size would suggest. Urshielle said something in a tribal dialect that Dante didn't understand. The other four, including Majala, then had a short back-and-forth in the same tongue. When they finished, the three assistants took their newest member away in the opposite direction.

Urshielle looked at Dante, caught his eyes, and moved toward him with purposeful but unhurried strides. Her demeanor was more than a little chilly but far from hostile or aggressive. As foreign as her background and environment were to him, she was still a human being. Dante would never have survived for so long if he hadn't learned to read people's feelings and intentions, no matter how stoic or poker-faced they were, regardless of cultural differences.

"Man," she addressed him. A conscious choice, he suspected, to use the most neutral and generic term she could think of. "It is unwise of you to be out of bed so soon. And it is not our normal custom to allow people from outside to watch our ceremonies."

The unspoken part of what she'd conveyed was that she had, for whatever reason, made an exception for him. He was almost glad she'd broached the subject since it was what he most wanted to ask her about.

He relaxed and pushed away from the column that had held him up. His already pale face turned even whiter, and his vision went black as he crumpled to the ground.

Sometime later, after he was safely back in bed and rested, Urshielle came in and sat beside Dante. "Raphorien said you wanted to speak to me."

"I'm sorry for breaking in on your ceremony. I was afraid you were going to kill her," he explained. "If I heard the oath correctly, you vowed to kill all Moonfiends. Why didn't you cut my throat or bash my head in after I fell unconscious the other night after the battle?"

She crossed her bare arms corded with lean muscle and shook her head. "The people of the Crescent do not mean to kill *all* Moonfiends. Only those who perpetuate the evil ways of moon-scraping and moon-plucking. Which is far too many of them. But, it would seem, not all."

"Oh?" He arched an eyebrow. Now was the time to let her speak rather than try to control the conversation himself. His direct nature made him want to bombard her with pointed questions and demand answers. Still, he was on unfamiliar turf, and he owed these people a debt of gratitude. It would be better to keep his mouth shut as much as possible and learn from what they had to say.

"Yes. We saw you fight against the Demorquens and fight well to save the last of the Harij. The Demorquens were taking advantage of what happened to their neighbors in ways that violated a treaty we made years ago, so I'd come to mediate.

"You were wounded in battle and risked your life. So we know that you were true to your word. This made me stay my hand. I brought you back here and left you in the care of Raphorien, the finest healer among our Crowned. That, if nothing else, seemed the fair and honorable thing to do."

Dante noted the ambivalence in her voice and demeanor. She had more she wanted to say, but due to her uncertainties, she was defaulting back to what must have been her normal way of inter-acting with outsiders—aloofness, coldness, a lack of interest in telling them anything important.

"You have my thanks. Raphorien did well. I'll have to tell him I'm sorry for putting too much strain on my leg."

As though ignoring what he'd said, Urshielle continued with the anecdote she'd begun a moment ago. "Most of the Harij women who survived the raid are now sisters among the Crescent-Kissed. I have spoken to all of them. Some were there in the belly of the compound when the metal man struck. So was Majala, who the Harij had enslaved."

Dante hadn't recognized her as such, but when infiltrating the facility, there had been poor lighting and little time to focus on faces. Besides, he suspected she'd been one of the enslaved people sleeping while the others pedaled the mounted bikes.

As for "metal man," he knew immediately to whom Urshielle referred. He was far more curious about what the women had told her.

Urshielle continued, "They said that you turned against your tribe on their behalf, that you fought against the metal man to stop the moon-scraping. It is...unfortunate that you failed. Still, we must express our gratitude for trying. You took injuries from the other Moonfiends before the fight against the Demorquens."

"I did try," he affirmed. "What you call moon-scraping is outlawed in the Stations, among my people. Some people, greedy rogues, keep doing it anyway. They lied to me. They told me that we were only there to collect precious materials from the quarry within the compound."

Urshielle grimaced. "I see. We owe you a debt of honor, no matter what. The other Kissed and I had seen the fire-angle of the Moonfiend ship and the lightning that told of them coming again, so I set out with two others. You did not see them, but they were there.

"We came to see if the Moonfiends once again meant to scrape and pluck. We did not find out about the Demorquen tribe until later. We were too late. The moon-scraping took place before we arrived. You stood in our place to oppose it. You could not succeed, but you did what was right. For that, we owe you."

Dante took in and processed all that she'd said. He didn't speak right away because he was unsure whether or not she meant that they owed him *beyond* saving his life. If the debt extended further than that, things were more complicated but also more promising.

Sensing his uncertainty, Urshielle clarified, "We must repay you. How do you wish to be repaid?"

"First of all, call me Dante. Second..." the sentence trailed off as his mind fixated on something she'd mentioned.

The *fire-angle* and the *lightning of the ship*. They sounded like superstitious nonsense but were pretty astute ways of putting it. She had to be referring to the trajectory of a descending shuttle and how they'd been able to track it by the glow it made upon entry into Earth's atmosphere. The flames blotted out sight for those within the craft.

As for "lightning," she likely meant the flash of adjustment thrusters. Particularly in cloudy or dusty weather, it might have looked like lightning to people on the ground.

The Dirtwalkers weren't stupid. He'd known this for a long time, but his appreciation for that fact had increased since encountering the Harij and the Crescent-Marked. They were "primitive" compared to the people of the Stations. Yet, the average Dirtside tribe member probably had to be sharper and cleverer than the average Atlantican, given how dangerous their lives were. Those lacking in intelligence would be among the first to be picked off by the planet's many hazards.

He cleared his throat. "It seems that you have a talent for noticing when a ship is coming down through the sky and determining where it will land. So, I would like you to help me locate the next one to descend in this area. Then I can board it, or take it for myself if I must, and return to what you think of as the moon. We call it the Atlantica Stations."

Urshielle smiled for the first time. It wasn't much of one, but better than nothing. "This we can do. It makes sense that you would wish to return home."

"Yeah, but more than that." His hands curled into fists. "When I return, I intend to settle my account with SSS—the 'tribe,' you might say, who betrayed me. When I deal with them, I will also see that moon-scraping and moon-plucking stop forever."

He meant it. Atlanticans were supposed to have stamped out o-harvesting and t-harvesting. Whatever power he had to make that true in practice, he intended to exercise it. Fully and without restraint.

Urshielle stared into his eyes for a full minute. Something within her changed. It was incredibly subtle but undeniable. "Very well. Dante."

CHAPTER FOURTEEN

Looking at Grind, Nasreen decided that he was only *pretending* to be still asleep.

They'd woken up together and chatted for roughly twenty minutes, snuggling and procrastinating about preparing for a long day's work. Then Grind had drifted back off to sleep since it was well before the time they *had* to arise. Or so it had seemed.

They'd ended up in his rented compartment at a hostel of sorts. It lay in the peripheral zone between the semi-respectable part of the Unders and the slums. Most of the other members of Reavo's crew had retired to compartments within the same building, but fortunately, Grind's was in the far corner with a bit more privacy than the others.

That was certainly a good thing, given how much noise they'd made. Nasreen knew she was taking a serious risk by sleeping with a man she'd barely met. Furthermore, he was part of a dangerous band of probable criminals whom she would have to spend time with afterward.

She'd needed the release. And the attention and affection. It didn't hurt that as she'd suspected, Grind knew what he was doing. Everything about him suggested a long history of showing women a good time.

And yet, she wondered.

She wondered if the handsome, charming man who'd expressed such healthy and flattering interest in her was interested in Nasreen Joelle or only in Kara Hengst. It was true that Kara existed because Nasreen had willed her into being and that most of Kara was identical—or at least highly similar—to Nasreen. As such, maybe it didn't matter. Despite the mild changes in appearance and affectations of personality, the fake persona of Kara *was* the real woman that Nasreen knew herself to be.

Still, the whole point of taking on the mantle of Ms. Hengst was to disguise herself. There would've been no need to invent Kara if Nasreen, the real Nasreen, was acceptable.

She frowned and silently told herself to shut up and stop being ridiculous. When portraying herself as no one other than Nasreen, she still got plenty of positive attention. The need to hide within the costume known as Kara was only to infiltrate the shuttle crew as someone with a clean record. It was professional, not personal. There was nothing wrong with Nasreen under normal circumstances.

Rubbing her eyes and sitting up in bed, she speculated on how long it might be until "normal circumstances" were a thing she would get to experience. Perhaps not too long, if everything on the job went according to plan.

Then again, normality bored her.

She went through the motions of preparing for the day, making tea for both of them, and taking a quick but thorough hot shower. She kept her clothes near the stall as she washed, on the off chance that Grind might try to poke through them for anything of interest.

As Nasreen shut off the water and wrung out her hair, she cursed herself for thinking that way. It was nearly impossible for her to completely shift out of the suspicious, cautious, borderline paranoid mindset that years of spy work had cultivated within her normal, day-to-day mental processes.

A notion or two had wormed into her thoughts over the last half-hour. The haze in her brain had lifted. The effects of alcohol, sleep, and excitement vanishing had allowed her to reflect and contemplate a little more.

Grind, she began to suspect, hadn't seduced her purely for fun. Sure, he'd enjoyed himself, as had she. Little things began to add up, though. Spending time with her was part of his duties as a crew member.

Nasreen used a macro-sponge on her hair, then stepped in front of the dryer and let it blast away the last of the hot water. Dressing once again in her clothes—or, rather, in Kara's clothes —she wondered how she could've been stupid enough to miss it last night.

She'd had to deal with a lot of information at once. She was nervous. Despite her expertise, ingratiating herself with a bunch of cutthroats was never exactly a relaxing thing to attempt. There was the alcohol, of course. The main reason Grind slipped through a crack in her defenses was simpler than that.

Namely, it was because she hadn't expected such a subtle ploy from these people. Captain Reavo had been arrogant and obnoxious, unashamedly straightforward about her abrasiveness. It suggested the woman relied upon sheer aggression to resolve her personnel problems. Nasreen had underestimated her.

Grind was her henchman. If he'd found anything out or suspected anything, Nasreen might've compromised her position as the crew's new pilot.

There wasn't much time to back out. Soon, they would be sailing Dirtside, where no one would be around to help if things turned nasty with Reavo and her flunkies.

When she returned to the compartment's main living area,

Grind was up, sipping a cup of tea and eating a nutritional biscuit. "Good morning, beautiful." He looked her up and down.

She flashed him a tired, half-appreciative smile before fetching a cup for herself and sitting beside him. "I never look *that* beautiful in the morning, but thank you for saying so anyway. Did you sleep well? I think I got twisted around wrong. Something in my shoulder is tight. Hurts a little."

Grind shrugged. "I'm fine. Is that going to affect your ability to fly? I can handle steering and other basic things, but it's always nice to have a real pilot on hand. It frees up the rest of us to do the other important stuff."

She nodded. "Ah, well, I'm glad I'm not the only one who knows *anything* about flying."

He chuckled. "You don't spend as much time as we do on that thing without learning how it works. Speaking of which, we ought to get you out there so you can familiarize yourself with the controls before it's showtime. Oh, Reavo wanted me to ask you. How do you feel about staying with the ship? You seem like the adventurous type." He smirked. "It's too bad we're only hiring you for the boring stuff."

Nasreen had already been processing the information he'd given her—the fact that her role as a pilot wasn't *entirely* necessary. Reavo had said something about being able to handle the ship reasonably well, too. Which meant that "Kara" was, in theory, expendable.

Asking her to stay onboard might mean they didn't want her snooping around while they collected their payload from Old Atlantica. In which case either their raid was even less legal than she'd thought...or simply that Grind was testing her to see how she reacted. To determine if she would object to following them around on their mission. Or perhaps to see if she seemed too eager to be left alone with the ship's logs and the crew's onboard personal effects.

"That's fine," she said. "It all pays the same, and frankly I'd rather not risk too much of my skin. I think I heard that they have Nightmutts in the Northeastern Sprawl. So if you don't need me to deal with them, I'm happy to guard the ship."

He leaned back in his seat and folded his hands behind his head. "Good. Now, let's get ready to go, shall we? Reavo isn't too much of a ball-buster about protocol and shit when we're *not* working, but she has a short temper when someone's late for an important job."

Nasreen stood and finished her tea. "I thought she had a short temper over *everything*, but maybe I haven't seen the worst of it yet." She let a twinkle creep into her eye, flashing it at him to show that she was only joking around. His reaction would be instructive.

As she'd suspected, Grind laughed in a good-natured way. There was an edge to it, an undertone that she disliked. He'd looked away and closed his eyes to avoid too much scrutiny of his face. What didn't he want her to see?

"Oh, you haven't." He sighed. "And if you're lucky, you won't. Just do what you're getting paid for, and everything will be fine."

She made a show of exhaling and relaxing her shoulders, a feint of relief. "Well, that's encouraging."

In fact, it was the opposite. The warning was clear. They suspected *something*. They weren't sure what, but Grind had pegged her as someone hiding her true motivations from them.

Since Grind and Reavo could probably wrestle the shuttle through space at least well enough to get into the Stations' artificial orbit and call for help, if nothing else, they could still expect to return home with their nice fat payload. Possibly without having to share it with their new, excessively curious pilot.

Should things go sideways, Nasreen needed an angle. A way to even the odds. She knew she could find one. There were always ways. Still, the job had become more complex, more hazardous.

Giving no hint about her fears, she stretched her legs briefly. "Okay. Let's go."

"Dante!"

The voice was sharp and held an imperative note of urgency. Not to the extent that the person calling for him thought she could boss him around, but she wanted to get his attention and didn't have the time to wait for him to make up his mind about it.

Dante looked up from the old book he'd been reading while basking in the afterglow of his simple workout. "What is it?" The woman hadn't stated that she wanted him to come with her, but he would be surprised if she didn't. He threw the sheet off his body and prepared to swing his legs down at a moment's notice.

The messenger was one of Urshielle's warriors, a young woman he frequently saw patrolling the halls or running messages and errands back and forth across the old hospital building. The crescent scars on her face were fully healed but probably hadn't been there for too long.

She waved her free left hand at him and drew it back in a beckoning motion. Her right hand clutched an oversized knife or short sword, a basic but useful weapon for the close-quarters environment of the building.

"We have seen a ship. Urshielle wishes to speak to you." She stood, halfway hesitant, a step or so over the door's threshold, as though prepared to come in and help him out of bed if he requested it or it seemed necessary but would prefer to give him the option to handle things himself.

Dante didn't waste time trying to negotiate such things. He pivoted so his hips turned without having to move his trunk or shoulders much to reduce the strain on his still-bandaged chest and back. Then he used his arms to brace his weight against the bed while shifting his legs over the edge, allowing his good leg to take most of the impact with the floor.

Standing up carefully but quickly, he grabbed the old hospital gown hanging on the lower-left bedpost. He threw it around his shoulders before sliding his feet into the available slippers. He'd been wearing nothing but his trunks and felt he should be a little more prepared. Yet putting on his actual clothes would take too long. Beyond any doubt, Urshielle didn't want him to keep her waiting.

Dante hobbled over to the young woman. By feeling the way his body moved and paying attention to the mechanics and pain signals, he crossed the room with relatively impressive speed despite his half-crippled condition. "I'm ready. Take me to her."

Nodding, the Crescent-Kissed girl turned and marched back out into the hallway. After a moment, she slowed her brisk pace to something more moderate so Dante could keep up. He had to admit that he appreciated the gesture. The unnatural gait he'd adopted took more out of him than walking normally. Being bedridden for days meant that his overall physical condition was somewhat below peak.

It occurred to him that he'd seen other patients being pushed around on stretchers or in wheelchairs. He *could* have requested one of those. It wouldn't be any slower, and it would've been easier on him.

That would only mean his fitness and strength would further degrade. He'd rather keep in *some* kind of shape, even if it was difficult, and put unusual types of strains on his body and read-just once he healed.

As they moved to the second floor's opposite end, Dante queried, "When did you spot the ship?"

"Only minutes ago," said the woman. "Urshielle thought you should know at once."

He nodded. "I will have to thank her for that."

Dante had been to the building's far side one other time since his arrival. A former sitting room lay there, but the Crescent-Marked had converted it into a crude observatory. The broad windows looked out over an expanse of sky that was largely unobstructed by other, taller buildings or natural impediments. They didn't have a fully panoramic view, but at least it allowed them to keep watch on the parts of the firmament above the more central and populous sections of the island. The Crescent commune lay near the fringe of the Sprawl, not far from a rocky western coastline.

His escort opened the door and stood holding it. He inclined his head in thanks and limped in.

Urshielle was there with two other Kissed warriors and two healers, one of whom Dante instantly recognized as Raphorien. They stood in a rough semicircle around an old-fashioned telescope they'd mounted to look out through the window. There was also a small skylight they'd seemingly installed themselves by simply cutting a square out of the ceiling and adding a glass pane to it with some rough but serviceable reinforcement materials.

Urshielle stepped forward. "Dante. Come here and look through this device. You moon-people may have tools greater than this, but this leftover from the older days of the Earth is still functional for our purposes."

He strode over, trying to keep his movements as smooth as possible. "I know what it is. I'm glad you could get it to work." He wanted to ask more, to drill them with questions about what they'd seen and when, and how much resemblance it bore to other ships they'd seen descending toward Old Atlantica. Still, it would make more sense to trust their experience while looking for himself.

As he approached the telescope, he noted the weather conditions. It was late afternoon, heading toward evening. There was still daylight, but it was waning fast. The air was mostly clear but a tad damp and misty.

From what he could recall, this had been the island's standard climate before disaster struck. Atlantica's weather still lapsed into its old ways between bouts of dryness, dust storms, and weird electromagnetic activity in the tainted atmosphere that clung to the planet.

Grunting, he put his eye to the lens and looked.

It took him a second or so to comprehend what he saw. He'd used telescopes of this sort once or twice, but it had been years. His brain was far more accustomed to the prismatic camera scanners on his old ship. At first, everything simply looked like a brownish-grey haze of mist and dust, shot through with orange daylight.

One of the Crescent-Kissed women told him, "Move it down and to your right, slowly and gently. The sky ship was moving in that direction."

Dante grasped the tube and did as she'd instructed. The scene shifted, at first jerkily, but then he smoothed it out once he got a feel for the telescope's degree of sensitivity. He found a dial and zoomed out slightly, taking note of a faint reddish glowing object like a comet but slower streaking down through the sky to the east.

He zoomed back in on it. It was distant and distorted, but there was no mistaking it. The flame effect and overall appearance were that of a mid-sized, relatively standard Raider shuttle. People from the Stations were coming to the island for their usual purposes.

He wondered who they were.

Drawing back from the lens and staring out the window, Dante asked, "Have you been able to calculate where they're landing?"

Raphorien responded, "We believe so. They seem to be heading toward what we call the Gape Mouths. It is a part of the city where the ground collapsed into the pits and tunnels that once ran beneath Atlantica before much of the city rose into the sky at the Moonfiends' behest."

"How far?" Dante pressed on. The shuttle wasn't close enough for him to be optimistic that they could reach the landing site before dark.

Urshielle told him, "Two or three hours on foot. I can have a war party ready to escort you in ten to fifteen minutes."

Dante inhaled deeply through his nose and stared at the red speck in the sky, which was becoming visible even without the telescope. "Sounds good. Let's do it."

Raphorien looked at him, blinking and furrowing his brow with concern. "It would do you well to rest here another week or two." He sighed. "That could easily turn into another year or two, or decade or two, I suppose."

Dante gave the man a sad smile. Raphorien's kindness wasn't something he would forget. "Yes. I know it's risky. But the time to take that risk is *now.*"

CHAPTER FIFTEEN

Dante was secretly relieved when the ride ended near the edge of the so-called Gape Mouths, and he had no choice but to try to walk again. The flush in his cheeks and burning ears hadn't entirely abated during the whole of the trip.

Urshielle raised her hand. "Stop. This is where we must all go on foot. Majala, you have done well."

Dante looked up at the girl, the newest recruit among the Crescent-Kissed whom he'd tried to "rescue" from her induction into their order. The scars on her cheeks were still bright pink and partially scabbed over.

She bowed her head a notch or two. "Thank you, sister Urshielle." Her voice came in short, hollow gasps since she was out of breath from the exertion of pushing a cart for so long.

"No, thank *you*," Dante told her. He swung his legs over and slid off the cart onto the ground, bracing himself against the seat with one hand to absorb some of the impact and briefly loosened himself up with shakes and stretches. His wounds felt stiff and dully ached even though Majala had done all the work for most of the trip—at Urshielle's insistence.

The girl turned the cart around. One other, a more experienced sister, would accompany her for safety in case hostile tribespeople ambushed them. Or worse things. After dark, the possibility of attack by Atlantica's non-human denizens became far greater.

Dante watched them jog off down the street. He had to admit it was probably for the best that they'd gone to the trouble of saving his strength from early depletion. He might need all the stamina he had for whatever lay ahead. Still, he wasn't used to being carted around like some pampered aristocrat or spoiled child.

Urshielle stepped toward him with one strong, bony hand wrapped around the haft of her spear, the butt of which she planted on the ground by her feet as a show of authority. "Come. Follow us. Stay close, and be as silent as you can. The sky ship has probably landed within the Mouths.

"When the earth collapsed into the strange tunnels from the Old World, it exposed many buried things. Some of which the Moonfiends collect for plunder or whatever they do. This is likely why they came."

"Yeah," was all Dante could say. He tried to keep an open mind about who might be aboard the shuttle they'd sighted. It was unwise to cling too strongly to one particular possibility when uncertain. There was too much danger of getting mentally prepared for a given scenario and being shocked into inaction or stupid mistakes when it turned out to be something entirely different.

Still, he doubted the ship could be much of anything other than a lower-grade or medium-grade gang of Marauders or perhaps the less confrontational sorts of Reapers. The Dirt-walkers seemed to regard the Gape Mouths as an accursed place, so there wouldn't be much human harvest. Whoever had come down to the planet were most likely scavengers after cheap and easy salvage.

Urshielle turned and led the way toward a partially destroyed subway entrance. With her in front were three other warriors, two with rifles and one with a spear like their leader's. Dante fell into the middle of the pack. Another four women brought up the rear. One had a pistol, one a short sword, and the other two had polearms.

He wondered if the Crescent-Marked had recovered any pulsecore weapons. It was doubtful, but if so they probably stored them back at their headquarters as secret weapons of last resort, too precious to waste on run-of-the-mill activities.

Dante had his knife and his razorfist. He could defend himself at close range. If anyone started shooting at them from a distance, they would have to all hide and flee, or he would need to rely upon the skills of the two riflewomen.

He asked Urshielle, "Do you know all the paths through this place? It sounds like your people don't come here often."

"No," the leader admitted. "We know the general lay of the land. I have been through about half of it on a rescue mission. We can navigate it well enough to find this ship. But we must rely upon our wits and reflexes no matter what."

Dante grunted. Everything he knew from bitter experience inclined him to agree with the tall woman's statement.

It was dark by now. Earth was usually windier during the day, but a strong night breeze was picking up. Normally they would avoid it by going underground. Where they were going was a physical paradox—it was neither above the surface nor truly subterranean.

When the bulk of Atlantica Metro—centered on the wealthy downtown business district and the more populous and influential suburbs—had been scooped out of the Earth and elevated to the stars, it left an enormous crater in the middle of Atlantica's southern plain.

The devastation it caused was widespread and almost awe-inspiring. The roofs of subway tunnels, basements, and sewers had collapsed as the masses of concrete, steel, and crystal around them had torn themselves asunder. Pipes and bundles of wiring had been ripped from the ground, cutting jagged lines through labyrinthine infrastructure that had taken decades to build.

What was left was the Gape Mouths, the outskirts of the central crater. They were artificial badlands, a series of manufactured ravines and canyons and interconnected rubble pits that extended from the great depression like cracks surrounding a hole in some glass.

The Crescent-Kissed had voiced their belief that the shuttle had probably landed in one of two areas. One was right at the edge of the crater where there would be more space. The other was atop a noticeable hill or pyramid of debris about halfway between the pit and the edge of the Mouths, where there would be more clearance. Dante was inclined to agree.

He trusted the women's expertise. Still, as they descended the subway ramp toward the darkened labyrinth's western periphery, a primitive feeling of dread rose in his breast. It was like passing through the gates of hell. Or, in a way, like going Dirtside to begin with. The Mouths were nearly as much a different world relative to the surface as the surface was to the Stations.

Since it was a ramp rather than a staircase, Dante could traverse it with relative ease. He still had to favor his leg more than he liked, but he didn't fall behind. Ahead of him, the women on point ducked around the corner where the once-underground hall bent into the main subway platform area.

The platform was broad and empty. Its ceiling had ripped away in most places so the night sky's dim glow was visible but didn't penetrate far into what was otherwise a pitch-black environment. Dante still had his sphere, and its power cell retained at least a week's worth of juice, but he'd rather not draw attention by having a glowing ball floating amid them.

Something rustled up above. Everyone stopped at once. Dante was grateful that his companions had senses as sharp as his. It had sounded like something pushing off from a rubble-strewn surface at ground level, but it was hard to be sure. Then came a heavy but muffled *thud,* up ahead toward the mouth of another corridor that led away from the platform.

Dante said nothing. The Crescent-Kissed sisters exchanged glances but didn't offer their opinions. They merely waited and listened.

After a moment, Urshielle motioned for them to continue. They jogged across the wide floor, dodging the debris of Atlantica's ruined underground, and made for the side hall that led deeper into the maze. By now, Dante was starting to feel the exertion of moving quickly while half-crippled. His stamina was considerable, but there was no *easy* way to do this.

Passing into the corridor, they came to a room off to the side whose wall had partially collapsed. Dante glanced into the recess, but it was too dark to see anything. Nonetheless, he kept watch as they moved beyond it.

Then there was another sound behind them. A faint rush of air, followed by a heavy object striking something near the edge of the collapsed street over their heads and possibly sliding off. Yet there was no impact noise.

The sisters slowed down, and he caught their gazes, noting the trepidation. If they knew anything, they weren't yet revealing it, but their worry was too obvious for him to automatically dismiss the worst possibilities out of hand. There were too many chances that it *wasn't* the sound of falling debris.

A minute or two later, Dante felt it, *sensed* it, again. He couldn't see, hear, or smell the person or creature, whatever it was, but he knew it was there. His certainty came from various subtle things, cues that most human beings missed when separated too long from the rigors of daily survival.

The Crescent-Kissed women sensed it, too. A faint but perceptible increase in tension and unease showed as an electric signal passed between them, warning one another that all was not well.

Dante casually turned and looked behind him. He did it somewhat fast, but not suddenly or abruptly. It was such a fluid, natural movement that its very lack of haste might have been what made the difference.

The *thing* following them realized he'd spotted it and slinked into the pool of shadows within the broken chamber along the hall. He saw it for only a tiny fraction of a second. In that brief time, he saw enough.

Their pursuer wasn't human. It was too big and ungainly, and the way it moved and carried itself suggested an animal that preferred to go on four legs. Yet it had been resting on its haunches and had walked on two legs into the room, falling back into a quadrupedal stance right as it vanished from sight.

The sister to his left was suddenly at his side, panting and glancing around. "What did you see? I saw only a moving shadow."

Dante exhaled and cleared his throat, giving his brain a second to process the new information and his body the same amount of time to prepare for battle. "Nightmutt. A big one. I'm not sure what kind."

There were no specific *kinds* that he was aware of. Each Nightmutt was more or less unique. Their only common traits were that they were hideously mutated and incredibly dangerous.

Urshielle hissed, "You are certain? *Certain?*"

"As certain as I can be," he affirmed. "It hid in that room back there, probably hoping we'll keep going and it can sneak back up behind us."

The sisters' leader moved forward, her motions swift and sleek. "No. We must not allow it. If it wishes a confrontation, let it happen now at our choosing. The Nightmutts often trail their prey to make them afraid until they do something stupid. Instead, we must fight them while our courage still holds. There are enough of us, and we are well-armed. Come!"

She gestured, and the women fell into position. Those armed with spears were in the center, and those with rifles were in the wings. Dante found himself rear and center, next to the copper-haired woman with the sword and the dark-braided woman with the pistol.

He would've preferred to find a more defensible position. They could lead the creature on a little longer and lure *it* into *their* trap. However, they had only the vaguest idea of what lay ahead in the ruins. Urshielle might have been right. He bit his tongue and flexed his fingers within the sheath of his razorfist.

The group moved toward the room where the Nightmutt had taken refuge. Since they hadn't searched the chamber, they didn't know if there was another way out, and the creature had fled somewhere else. They all seemed to doubt it as much as Dante did. It was hiding, not running. The darkness beyond the collapsed wall was total, a thick mass of blackness that nearly possessed a substance of its own.

Dante cursed the fact that no one had brought a crossbow. Taking on a Nightmutt with melee weapons was an extremely dicey proposition. Guns would make enough noise to give away their presence. Sure, the Raider crew might assume it was random Dirtwalkers shooting at each other. But if they were anywhere nearby and had any sense, gunshots would put them on their guard no matter what.

Total silence settled over the canyon-like hallway as they approached. The night wind over their heads seemed too distant to be of consequence. There were only the ever-so-soft footfalls of the nine humans, creeping toward the thing that awaited them in the dark.

Something *crashed*. The point women tensed and bared their teeth, weapons ready. Dante sensed at once that something was wrong. The sounds weren't moving *toward* them.

Light and shadow shifted. Movement flickered off to the left at the corner of Dante's vision. By the time he pivoted toward it, his chest coming afire with pain as he strained the damaged muscles, the Nightmutt was barreling toward them from somewhere in the collapsed mass beyond the room. It had found another way out and flanked them.

The sisters screamed, a mixture of terrified alarm and determined battle cry. When they formed words, it was in a language of their own that Dante didn't know. He gritted his teeth and braced himself, leaning into the invisible barrier of his sudden, primordial terror.

The Nightmutt was the size of a pony or perhaps a small bear. Its shoulders and front section were shaggy with fur, and in the faint light, Dante glimpsed small pointed ears, more like a pig's than anything, and dangling jowls.

Its hindquarters didn't look mammalian. It had back legs like a frog—powerful enough to launch it high into the air. That was how it had kept up with them while making only two or three movements.

The woman with the rifle aimed and fired. The shot rang out, the *crack* echoing multiple times through the angular expanse, and light and fumes rose from the gun's muzzle. At the same instant she squeezed the trigger, the Nightmutt had leapt. It intended to clear the last distance between them with a single massive bound.

Dante couldn't tell if the shot hit. There was no time. The massive creature sailing through the air like something far lighter was about to crash down right in the middle of the group. On top of him.

His brain raced, and his body tried to keep up. He had a fraction of a second to swing aside on his good leg and maybe enough time to—

The Nightmutt landed. Dante somehow launched himself aside and swerved back, his upper body narrowly avoiding the creature's broad, powerful claws. On the return swing, he punched his razorfist toward the monster's shoulder, feeling the impact as the blade within sheared through hair, hide, and bone. It wouldn't have gone deep enough to kill, but it was a good strike.

The Nightmutt roared, sounding like an uncomfortable mixture of a bellowing ox and a croaking frog, and tried to smash Dante with its foreleg. The knife wound to the shoulder stopped it from doing so. As it tried to thrash away, Dante huddled closer to it, gagged at the foul stench of its matted fur, and dragged the blade laterally along its torso, shearing through a powerful rib.

Then the Kissed women moved in, snarling in rage. Their spears thrust into the beast from multiple directions. The Nightmutt lashed out with its good forepaw, gnashed its jaws, and tried to kick with its rear legs. One of the frog-like feet caught the copper-haired swordswoman in the chest, *crunching* bones and making her spit up blood as she fell.

Dante swiveled under the monster. It was the best way to stay out of easy reach of its limbs while getting closer to its underbelly, and the spears kept the creature from simply running off in any direction. Straining against the blaze of pain in his chest, he sliced open the Nightmutt's lower breast and upper abdomen. Blood and viscera poured out, which he dodged as the creature groaned and convulsed.

Urshielle pounced forward and drove her spear into the Nightmutt's eye. It shuddered one last time and fell over on its side with a wet, heavy *thud*.

Dante got to his feet. Blood was all over his arms and shoulders. His wounds were screaming with pain. Two sisters had rushed over to check on the woman who got kicked.

"She's dead," one reported, her face drawn and grave. "Her whole chest was crushed."

Urshielle was panting as she wiped off her spear on the beast's fur. She shook her head. "We will honor her when the time is right when we return this way. We must move on. She died helping us to remove this abomination from the world. It will threaten no one else. Now, go. That way."

They paused briefly to pull the dead woman's shawl over her face, a token of respect until they could deal with her properly. Dante hobbled along at the center of the group again. The brief, savage fight against the Nightmutt had strained his injuries, and his chest was bleeding again. He ignored it for now since the flow seemed minimal. If he could get back to the Stations, he could find a way to get medical care.

Urshielle led them in the general direction of the debris hill they'd spotted earlier. They passed through long lengths of subway tunnels and climbed through pipes that acted as short-cuts between walls, keeping to the shadows when the sky's dim light threatened to expose their silhouettes.

When the rubble pile came into sight, rising from amid a mini-crater like a parody of the great one where the city's bulk had been, Dante spied the low glow of idling boosters and interior illumination before he made out the undeniable outline of a mid-range cargo shuttle.

They all halted, hugging the wall, and watched in silence. So far, nothing was moving, aside from barely visible indications of motion within the cockpit.

Urshielle touched Dante's arm. "What do you plan to do? How will you speak to them? They are your fellow Moonfiends, but do you have any guarantee that they will be friendly?"

He smiled grimly. "None. But I know how to deal with people like this. They trade useful things. They respond to bribes and threats. I'll bargain for my passage. I can help them with what-ever their mission is, pay them back when we return to the Stations if need be." He sighed. "They *might* accept my offer."

The glum look on the warrior woman's face suggested that she wasn't optimistic. "You know these people better than I do. Yet, doubt fills me. If they are like the ones we have encountered, plunderers and thieves and murderers, they might simply try to kill you and take your things. Let me and my sisters wait in hiding nearby. We can fight them if they do not listen to you."

Dante wasn't sure how to respond at first. They'd already lost one of their people to get him here. "You shouldn't need to do that. I can talk my way onto the ship. I've dealt with people worse than they probably are."

If they were "average" raiders, that would be true. He had no way of knowing until he met them face-to-face.

To his surprise, Urshielle chuckled at the response. There was a cynical edge to it, but it wasn't entirely unkind.

"You are many things, Dante," she stated. "A brave warrior, a man of honor, and perhaps an outcast among your people. But a charming teller of smooth tales, a hustler...this you are not."

It wasn't in his nature to bother trying to disagree. He only shrugged.

She added, "We will keep our spears ready, I think. Now, go. Good luck."

CHAPTER SIXTEEN

Captain Reavo didn't look particularly happy to see her new pilot. Not that Nasreen was much surprised. Reavo generally didn't seem pleased about much of *anything*, as near as she could tell.

"Hey! Kara, whatever your last name is, I forget. Where the fuck were you?" The small woman stomped across the loading bay, adjusting her hat as she moved, her jaw thrust forth in a simian display of dominance and intimidation. "We could have already been hitting the dirt by now!"

Nasreen smiled. "I was the same place Grind has been. You wouldn't want to leave without him, would you? I made sure to bring him along."

Grind was beside her, and he flashed a mischievous grin that was supposed to *look* surreptitious. Although everyone could see it. He must have a reputation with the ladies. Nasreen could only imagine the jokes that got bantered around the drinking table.

Reavo made a show of glaring at Grind. "Quit wasting my pilot's time, Grind. We got a schedule to keep here!" She flung her hands at him in a strange gesture. Nasreen couldn't tell if it was an actual signal or simply a bizarre habit of the captain's.

While Grind smirked, Nasreen glanced at the big clock on the wall. "We're two minutes earlier than the time you gave us. Don't worry, Captain, we have all day and all night to complete the job, don't we? It won't take me long to familiarize myself with your ship. We covered that last night."

One of the men in the crowd behind Reavo laughed and shouted, "What's that stupid old saying? 'Being on time is late, and being early is on time.' Some crap like that? Ha, ha."

He was half chiding Nasreen and half poking fun at his boss. Nasreen wasn't sure how smart the latter was since Reavo was getting a sullen, nasty look in her eyes that was probably more dangerous than her usual bluster. It was the look of a woman who was determined to find a target for her anger soon. One way or another, she wanted to hurt someone.

"Well, get over here and get started, then. The sooner we leave, the sooner we get paid." She stood and folded her arms. "All of us."

Nasreen strolled past her and ducked into the side hatch of the shuttle, with Grind languishing behind. He didn't follow her in but waited outside, mingling with the bulk of the crew. No doubt he had reports to give on everything he'd learned about the so-called Kara Hengst.

Nasreen had been careful, though. Any information he'd picked up on her was either stuff she had *allowed* him to find or irrelevant trivia. She'd gone into this mission without any loose ends dangling in the breeze.

Within the shuttle, four men had taken up positions, mostly in the combination cargo and seating chamber in the back. One had conveniently positioned himself in the cockpit so he could watch Kara as she slid into the pilot's chair. She ignored him for the time being and looked over the cockpit, console, and all the miscellaneous gadgetry.

None of it was new or strange to her. The exact configuration was slightly different from what she was used to, and she intended to ask a question or two just to make it look like she was taking the job seriously enough to double-check such things. Otherwise, provided the ship was in proper working order, she expected no problems.

At least, not of a mechanical nature.

It was impossible to dismiss the suspicion that Reavo, Grind, and the others were setting her up. Not merely in the sense of planning to screw her out of her share of the pay, but that they might be trying to entrap her specifically so they could draw out the client's little conspiracy against them. If that was the case, they might take her to some godforsaken corner of the ruins on Earth and torture her for information.

She tried not to shudder in a brief moment of anxiety, a sense of disbelief about why she allowed herself to wind up in situations like this. There were easier ways for a girl to get her thrills in life.

Someone came over to her seat. She didn't look up to see who it was, but judging by the sound of the movements and the overall vibe she got, it had to be Grind. She had long ago refined the art of recognizing people based on minimal stimuli.

His hands descended onto her shoulders. His fingers felt good against them, but the unease in the pit of her gut remained.

"Kara, a little warning," he said. "Reavo's about to do a weapons check. She's not planning to give you a gun because as our pilot your role is to stay with the ship. Don't take it personally. The captain might get upset if you make an issue out of it."

Nasreen swallowed. "What if a Nightmutt shows up while I'm staying with the ship? I can't try to drive it off?"

He shrugged. "We won't be going far from the shuttle. A Nightmutt would attack us before it bothered with a big hunk of metal. Don't worry about it."

Nasreen had two concealed weapons, a mini-pulsecore pistol in her boot and a wrist knife in her sleeve. The latter was similar to a razorfist but smaller and more discreet. The blade ejected beneath the hand at wrist-joint level, making it harder to use but easier to conceal, relative to the overhand "punching" operation of a typical razorfist.

Reavo might find them and strip them from her. In which case, she would have to find other ways of protecting herself.

Minutes later, the captain and the rest of the crew boarded. "Weapons!" Reavo barked, hands on her hips.

Three men went to the armory and returned with crates filled with guns. A few pulsecores and older conventional firearms, but generally quality stuff from what Nasreen could see. Reavo's crew might not have been major players with top funding, but they had access to enough hardware that it was clear they weren't messing around.

Then the captain repeated to Nasreen what Grind had said, albeit less politely.

"Besides," she added, "we don't know if you *deserve* to handle our guns yet. Prove yourself, and maybe we'll trust you with one."

Nasreen put on her best Kara smile. "I'll try my best."

After that, it was all routine as the crew settled in, she and the captain reviewed coordinates and flight plans, and she, the pilot, powered up the shuttle.

Everything went smoothly. Nasreen thanked the powers that be that they hadn't frisked her for weapons, but they seemed savvy enough to guess that she probably had something on her person anyway, at least a knife. They probably figured their superior numbers and firepower would be enough to neutralize it if push came to shove.

On the downside, Reavo sat in the copilot's seat, where she continuously leaned over Nasreen's shoulder and tried to micromanage her flying.

"Hold it," she snapped. "You should be approaching faster now and slower later. Where did you learn to fly?"

In her pleasant Kara voice, Nasreen said, "At a flight school. But it's your ship, so I'll try to follow your suggestions."

It was hard not to tense when they penetrated the Earth's atmosphere, and the flames kicked up. It always happened, but it was a naturally disconcerting experience, especially when piloting a spacecraft that she didn't personally know inside and out. The shuttle held up, and soon they entered the lower atmosphere where gravity kicked in fully, and the worst of the interference dissipated.

Nasreen gestured at a holographic readout showing the exact location where they would land. It appeared to be an especially rugged and broken section of the old city's former suburbs. "Okay, the coordinates say that—"

"No," Reavo interrupted. "Don't go by the coordinates. I don't like this weather. There's more wind than we thought, and you don't seem like a good enough pilot to keep us from falling into that giant crater. Instead, head for...that outcropping or hill or whatever it is. There. See?"

Nasreen frowned as she followed the woman's pointing finger, then quickly readjusted the coordinates herself. "Yes, we can do that. Whatever you say."

Someone chuckled amid the crew in back. Watching and listening to the captain heckle the new girl was their entertainment for the flight.

The wind was stronger in the tropospheric altitudes, but Nasreen guessed it would lessen as they got closer to the surface. She calculated their trajectory well enough that the shuttle hovered down almost directly on top of what Reavo had called an outcropping. It was more like a miniature artificial mountain made of wreckage. The scooping-out of the original city had wrought severe havoc on the old structures, leaving a blasted expanse of gutted buildings, exposed tunnels, and pit-like basements.

The top of the great mound was relatively flat, perhaps due to settling over the decades. Nasreen wondered how stable it was. As the shuttle moved atop it, all that happened was that a few pieces of loose debris dislodged themselves and rolled downhill. Otherwise, the weird pyramidal structure held firm.

The shuttle stopped, and Nasreen put it in idle-hover. The engines quieted to a dull *thrum*.

Reavo immediately unstrapped herself and sprang to her feet. "Right. Could've been worse, I guess. Kara, stay. Everyone else, start unloading our shit. I don't want to be here all day. This isn't that kind of job. Just a simple run in, grab the stuff, and get out."

Nasreen obeyed, keeping silent and playing the role of the semi-experienced new crewmate who was simply glad to have succeeded at her primary task and was now basking in gracious relief.

In fact, she watched, listened, and waited.

There were mundane procedures pilots sometimes performed when idling—setting all the bells and whistles into low-power mode to save on fuel and batteries, that sort of thing. Nasreen made an unflashy show of doing all of the above while secretly working on her Plan B.

Reavo and her minions were distracted. They thought they'd corralled her well enough to ignore her for the moment, and they had work to do besides. No one paid too close attention as she removed a small side panel on the shuttle controls and began to work at one of the security chips with the point of her wrist knife.

A little-known weakness of this particular model was how easy said chips were to remove. Once they were gone, an individual with the right know-how and the right programs in their sphere, could hack into the ship's launch AI without much trouble. Nasreen pulled out her device and pretended to use it to double-check their flight path back while she ran the appropriate script in the background, pocketed the chip, and replaced the panel.

It only took a couple of minutes. When she finished, the shuttle was rendered inoperable for anything except slow surface-hovering until someone undid a specific key sequence lock. The crew's only options for getting off the planet now were to allow Nasreen to handle it or spend an inordinate amount of time trying to hack through her counter-security program and brute-force the code.

Either way, they weren't going to have an easy time dumping her body in this wasteland and skipping back home if that was their plan.

As Nasreen finished implementing her backup scheme, the unmistakable report of a rifle shot broke the air outside.

She froze, her alertness kicking up two or three notches. It sounded like the rest of the crew had done the same since all activity momentarily ceased. Then it resumed, with low voices muttering all around.

"...kilometer or so away," someone pointed out.

Another voice added, "Probably Dirtwalkers shooting each other over a scrap of dried rat skin or something."

Then Reavo's voice added, "Which means that Dirtwalkers might be massing nearby, you morons. Pick up the pace! We don't want to deal with them if we don't have to."

Nasreen got up from her seat and offered to help unload.

Reavo pointed at a box in the corner. "Yeah. Bring that out. Then wait by the hatch."

The box turned out to be a portable toilet. This kind unfolded into a stall large enough to house an above-average-sized man, then compartmentalized and ejected the waste before refolding itself. They were impractical in the civilized confines of the Stations but popular with workers and Plunderers who went Dirtside since the blasted hellscapes of Earth had no shortage of places for the things to be emptied.

Still, Nasreen was unsurprised that this particular piece of gear was what Reavo had assigned to her.

She carried it out of the shuttle and placed it on a solid spot near the hill's edge, next to various other pieces of mundane gear.

Then she waited near the threshold of the shuttle's main hatch, as the captain had instructed.

Looking out over the ruins of the Sprawl, Nasreen shuddered. The breeze was chilly. The sun had gone down right before they had arrived. It was the sight of the devastated metropolis with its seemingly endless pockets of darkness, desolation, and horror that made her so uncomfortable.

Suddenly it seemed as though the entire crew had surrounded her. As if on cue, they were all done with their work and happened to be standing around her in a circle. Several of the largest men were behind her inside the ship itself, of course. Reavo had taken up a position facing straight across from her.

This wasn't good. The moment of truth was approaching.

"So," the Captain jeered, swaggering a bit as the sullen anger she'd displayed earlier rose to the surface. "What's this I hear about you and Grind? You trying to turn my crew against me by getting them whipped?"

She phrased it as a joke, and half of her flunkies laughed, but Nasreen knew what it was. The opening salvo of what the small, belligerent woman *really* wanted to know.

Nasreen let her face break into a goofy smile. "Grind is an adult. He can make his own decisions without supervision, can't he?"

A few of the others, including Grind, chortled at that.

Reavo reflected the smile at her, but with a nasty twist that reminded Nasreen of a snarling rodent. "He didn't tell you that we lost our usual pilot at the last minute, did he? And you *just so happened* to show up at exactly the right time?"

Nasreen blinked furiously and let herself bristle, adopting a slightly hurt and put out look. The expression of someone innocent who is incensed at being wrongly accused.

"What? What do you mean? You put out an ad for a pilot, didn't you? I was looking for work, I saw the ad, and I responded to it right in time. What's wrong with that?"

"Sure," Reavo shot back. "Sure you did. So damn perfect. Even your act. Grind is a little confused about where you're from though, Kara Hengst. He said your accent changes a bit when you're excited. Weird, isn't it?"

Nasreen let her jaw drop. "What business of his is it to tell you things like that?" Her mock indignation made a decent cover for the terrible fear that they'd found her out, that she would never get off the planet without either fighting them off or having awful things done to her until she revealed who she was working for.

Grind shrugged and gave her a mildly apologetic look. "The crew's business is my business, and vice versa. Sorry, Kara. Or whatever your real name is."

Reavo abruptly drew a pistol. Nasreen almost pulled hers, but the captain didn't seem like she was about to fire it, only use it to threaten her. The other armed crew members could all draw on her as well. Nasreen might be able to blast Reavo to hell, which would give her *some* satisfaction, but she would outlive the captain by seconds at most.

Reavo sneered, "Yeah. You're not who you say you are, *Kara*. What's your real name? And who do you work for? Because it sure as hell isn't us. For every five seconds I don't get an answer, I blow off one of your limbs. Don't think you can get away with bleeding out. Murad here," she gestured at a gangly, dark-faced man beside her, "will get a tourniquet on it and keep you alive in time for the next one to go bye-bye. Get it? Now, I'm gonna start counting. One. Two..."

Nasreen quailed within. She wanted to collapse but didn't. She'd failed miserably to avoid this fate despite all her work. Even her Plan B wouldn't save her from such intense paranoia and straightforward brutality. Reavo was crazier and more ruthless than she'd thought.

"Three..."

The big bearded guy who'd hovered near the captain back at the bar grunted, "Boss! Someone's coming."

A shaft of what barely qualified as light fell from between the nighttime clouds overhead. It was a mixture of the moon's natural radiance and the unnatural light produced by the always-illuminated Atlantica Stations, which had supplanted the glow of the stars down on Earth.

In the center of the dim ray was a humanoid figure, probably a man. He was of middling height, lean, and wearing a long coat. He had his hands up by the sides of his head, palms facing outward, the universal gesture of one who means to show that he comes in peace and means no harm.

Everyone noticed him at once. It was as though he'd crept up unawares until then and selected that specific moment to unveil himself, to *allow* them to see him. Still, no one spoke for a second or two. All eyes turned to the captain.

Reavo's lip curled up from her teeth. Looking at her with growing revulsion, Nasreen grasped that she was in no mood to receive unexpected guests.

"Who the hell are you?" the small woman snapped. The fingers of her right hand curled and uncurled lightly around the hilt of her pistol.

The man took two slow, deliberate steps forward. He kept his hands in the air. "My name is Dante Shale. I'm a Marauder who got stranded here. I'm looking to hitch a ride back to the Stations since I don't feel like spending the rest of my life on this rock. I can make it worth your while. Whatever you're doing here, I can help."

Reavo snorted. "*You're* Dante Shale? For fuck's sake. I thought you'd be a little taller."

Nasreen scanned the archives of her mind. She'd heard the name. A well-known, well-regarded Marauder, he seemed to be somewhat of a celebrity among the social flotsam who went Dirtside, not to mention the working classes and lumpen types.

There was also a certain amount of buzz that he'd finally attracted the attention of high society and big business. His ventures did tend to be profitable.

Now that she could see the man better, he looked the part. As Reavo had crudely observed, he wasn't particularly tall. He otherwise had an air of rugged toughness about him, to the point that he looked downright dangerous if crossed. He'd been sick or injured recently, though. His face was wan, and bandages showed under his frayed clothes.

His light body armor was of relatively high quality, though. So too was the razorfist he wore over his forearm. It was the kind of thing a professional would outfit himself with. Other gear and gadgets hung from his belt or the inside of his jacket. If he had any guns on his person, Nasreen couldn't see them.

The moonlight, such as it was, caught his eyes. They flashed a brilliant, predatory green. There was a hyper-alertness in them, a readiness to act. Whatever the man felt behind his impassive mask, Nasreen couldn't properly call it *fear* as most people understood it.

Reavo's tension, already keyed up and ready to crack, rose another notch into the realm of barely contained hysteria. Her head snapped back and forth as she looked between the newcomer and her befuddled crew.

Someone behind Nasreen said gruffly, "I heard Dante Shale was dead. Just before we left, it was. Someone said he took on this big job for one of the solar companies and finally bit off more than he could swallow. Ended up right in the hornet's nest and the Dirtwalkers finally composted his ass."

Reavo glared at him, then the others. "What have the rest of you heard, exactly?" She turned to Nasreen. "What about *you?* You know this guy? Any idea why he's showing up right now, minutes after we landed like he knew our coordinates to begin with? *Huh?*"

Before Nasreen could respond, Dante, or whoever he was,

called, "I don't know any of you people. I was with some Dirtwalkers who had an old telescope. They let me use it to calculate where you'd be landing before they turned me out. I helped them against an enemy tribe, so they owed me that much, at least. All I want is a ride home."

One of the other women in the crew—Nasreen was pretty sure it was the girlfriend of the big bearded guy who'd been hanging onto Reavo's shoulder back in the bar—scoffed, "Since fucking when do Dirtwalkers have any sense of hospitality toward us? Hah! This is a load of shit, Reavo."

The captain was still staring at her new pilot. "Yeah, it is, isn't it, *Kara?* This guy is working with you. He jumps us when we least expect it, is that right? Or his stupid friends hired you to tell him where we'd be landing so he can sweep in and the two of you can steal our payload and our ship. It all makes sense now. I fucking knew it!"

"No," Nasreen insisted, "I've heard of Dante Shale, but I've never even seen—"

Reavo swiped her arm through the air as though physically cutting Nasreen off from speaking, and her arm came out of the gesture pointed at Dante, finger extended. "We'll deal with the mole in a minute. First, kill him!"

Everyone drew guns at once, and as Dante reflexively ducked sidelong back into the surrounding pools of shadows, Nasreen uttered the one phrase she could think of that summed up how badly the whole job had cocked up.

"Oh, *shit.*"

CHAPTER SEVENTEEN

"Oh, *shit!*" Dante growled, his eyes widening as the unpleasant little woman who seemed to be the Raiders' captain gave the order to shoot him. Everyone on the ridge above him drew their guns at once, three or four pulsecore weapons and a motley assortment of older combustion-cartridge pistols, shotguns, and short-barreled rifles. Although not a top-tier band, the smugglers were nevertheless well-armed.

Still, they were neither as fast nor as accurate with their guns as they could've been. He was out of sight by the time the shooting started. Bullets and pulsecore rounds streaked through the darkened air he'd vacated. By using his good leg as a fulcrum to launch his body in a series of quick lunging motions, he was able to get clear of the line of fire while also moving erratically enough to make himself a difficult target.

They couldn't see shit, he guessed. The residual light from the shuttle had impaired their night vision, and they would need a moment or two of staring into the blackness to see where Dante was.

As he stole down the rubble mound and into the jumbled floor-level waste beyond its base, he saw two other things. The blonde girl, the pilot, had broken free from the others and was sprinting toward the nearest corridor, trying to get away from the rest of the crew. The others were starting to pile in after her.

"Get her!" the captain shrieked. "Get her, get her!"

The other thing was the rustling shadows from around the periphery of the unnatural clearing. Urshielle and her sisters were moving in—the outbreak of violence had convinced them that Dante's attempt at negotiation must have been a disappointment.

He scampered across an open floor area, heading toward another, smaller pile of debris that looked like it would withstand lead bullets and a modest volley of pulsecore rounds. A final glance showed him something interesting. The Dirtwalkers had allowed the fleeing blonde woman to pass. They seemingly sensed that she wasn't one of the Raiders.

Then they sprang their attack.

Two rifle shots rang out and effectively vaporized the head of one of the Raiders. His decapitated body teetered over as the others ducked low, seeking cover or simply picking up speed as they ran after the pilot. Then the sisters with hand weapons moved in. Spears thrust and another raider screamed, skewered from two directions. In his death agonies, he hurled a short-barreled rifle into the air. It clattered on the ground about two meters from Dante's hiding spot.

The remainder of Reavo's crew began blasting at random into the darkness. Dante winced as one of the clumsy barrages caught another Crescent-Kissed woman in the chest, legs, and stomach, ripping her apart and knocking her against the far wall. The others melted into the shadows before any got hit.

The captain screamed in her abrasive, high-pitched voice, "Get Kara! Get her first. We can deal with these idiots later. You guys, stay where you are!"

Dante had crawled out to grab the fallen rifle. He wasn't sure who the captain referred to with her latter statement. Everything was too dark and chaotic. Once the gun was in his hands, he crawled back behind his cover and tried to figure out exactly what the hell was going on.

He peeked over the edge of the pile. The Raiders had left two men to guard the ship, and those two were mostly engaged in taking potshots at Urshielle's gunwomen. Neither party was managing to hit much of anything. Each time their guns went off, they succeeded only in blowing a chunk of concrete out of their opponents' cover or sending a bullet or two whizzing over their heads, keeping the skirmish at a solid stalemate.

He glanced to the sides. Off to his right, Urshielle crouched behind a sheet of thick metal propped against a broken wall. She seemed almost afire with aggressive energy, as though she wanted to charge the men and take the risk of attacking them both with only her spear.

They were distracted, so perhaps it wasn't as stupid an idea as it sounded.

Dante stared at her until she noticed him. Then he showed her the rifle he'd picked up so she knew he had a projectile weapon on him. He pointed at himself, then made a crude hand motion to indicate that he would duck forward, shoot one of the men, and take cover behind an old rusting engine block lying amid a mass of scrap.

Then he pointed at her and made a similar motion, suggesting that she should weave up the mound from the flank while Dante was distracting the shooters. Even with only a melee weapon, she had a good chance of taking out the second one.

She nodded. Dante looked back at the rubble mound and waited for another volley of fire between the guards and the Dirtwalkers. Then he charged.

When the two men realized there was movement-noise behind them, Dante already had the one on the left in his sights. The man swiveled, but not fast enough. The Marauder squeezed the trigger twice.

The gun barked and blazed, and at least one of the rounds found its mark. A guttural groan escaped the man as his upper body snapped back and he dropped his gun, freezing for a second before crumpling against the ship. Blood stained his clothes and armor with its wet sheen.

Then Dante ducked behind the engine block. His stabbed leg shrieked a painful warning, but he pretended not to hear it. The second of the two guards pivoted to shoot at him, missing by a half-meter or so as Urshielle dashed out to the other side and reached the base of the mound behind him.

Dante stayed put. The other Dirtwalkers took a couple more shots at the hill of debris. The guard realized he was on the verge of being outgunned and seized up in a panic. Dante swung his arms around the edge of his cover and took a single shot at the man. He didn't much intend to hit anything, and indeed he missed. It kept the guard distracted and pressed down, though.

Urshielle exploded onto the top of the hill. How she'd climbed all of it so swiftly, and without making much noise, Dante would've liked to know. Her spear pointed out, and her attack trajectory was well-chosen. The remaining guard almost jumped out of his skin as he swung his rifle toward her, but the polearm's blade skewered him through the chest before he got anywhere close to fighting back.

The Marauder nodded in grim satisfaction as Urshielle used the spear to hurl the man aside. He fell off the edge of the pile and rolled down it, dragging a few pieces of detritus with him, and was dead by the time he reached the ground below.

Dante inhaled and trotted toward the hill. His leg hurt terribly. He was used to ignoring pain, but he might need drugs to quell it soon. Otherwise, the immediacy and intensity could become impossible to ignore.

He slung the rifle over his shoulder and mostly used his arms and good leg to climb the mound. When he was about two-thirds of the way up, Urshielle leaned over the edge, climbed partway down, and reached out to help pull him the rest of the way up.

"Thanks," he grunted. He immediately looked over the ship. It was hovering idle, and the door was open. The Raider might still have someone, a pilot or another guard, lurking within, but he doubted it. He could probably walk in and take the vehicle for himself.

Urshielle gestured toward it. "The sky ship is yours. You must go now. The Moonfiends will be back soon, and we might not be able to hold them off. This is why you came here, is it not?"

Dante nodded. He knew she was right. Something bothered him, though.

The attractive young blonde woman with the Raiders. They had been harassing and threatening her when he'd first approached the shuttle. He had no idea who she was or what the argument had been about, aside from the nonsensical accusations from the obnoxious captain. He wondered if she deserved to be left behind here with the rest of them.

If he delayed, Urshielle's party might lose more people in the ensuing fight. They *didn't* deserve that after everything they'd already done for him.

Dante put a hand on Urshielle's lean, muscular arm. "Thank you." Then he walked past her into the ship, his razorfist poised to strike if any defenders within tried to jump out at him.

The ship's interior was about what he'd expected—average if a little dirty. A quick inspection revealed it was empty. There was an off chance that someone might be hiding, but he didn't have time to tear the craft apart looking for them if so.

Instead, he went to the cockpit. The chair was empty. The console glowed dully, indicating that it was functional but idling with everything else. He examined it and the other controls, trying to refresh his memory of how everything worked.

He wasn't a pilot by trade. Over the years he'd picked up enough from Am that he was confident in his baseline ability to manage the machine, but the deeper secrets and intricacies of flying were unknown to him. He wasn't familiar with any quirks of this particular shuttle model.

Still, he was fairly sure he could get out of Earth's atmosphere and somewhere into the Stations' orbit in one piece. He might not be able to dock at a particular location of his choice successfully. He could at least get to the point where, if nothing else, he could activate a beacon and hitch a ride with a rescue vehicle or passing transport of some sort.

Dante sat in the chair and ran his hands over the controls. Nothing happened.

He grimaced. Most shuttles made in the last ten or twelve years were reasonably similar, but there was no full standardization for how to operate their consoles. He tried moving the steering handles, pressing buttons, holding his fingers down on the touchscreen, and even saying "wake up" and "back online" aloud in case it was voice-activated.

The console didn't respond.

"Goddammit," he cursed. He ought to have known better. The Raiders could afford to leave the shuttle sitting there with its hatch open because they had a security system locking up the controls.

He pulled out his sphere and performed a basic program scan. The results indicated a security program was blocking the interface, but it failed to identify the exact software used or what hardware they'd tied it to.

Dante felt like steam was about to pour from his ears. He was so close to escaping from the dead planet and returning home, and now it seemed that a basic but obscure firewall would be the literal death of him.

He skimmed through applications on his sphere, finding one he'd installed about half a year ago. It chained together multiple scripts and AIs that could diagnose security programs and point the user in the right direction for what they'd need to hack it.

Running it through the scanner panel turned up a slight hodgepodge of results. A floating addendum mentioned that whoever had locked the console was using a homebrew program rather than a mass-produced corporate one. Therefore its degree of strength and complexity was anyone's guess.

It may or may not have been installed in front of a key sequence lock, as well. And trying to brute-force it could potentially trigger a self-destruct script that might fry the telemetry, rendering the vessel entirely inoperable.

Dante shut his eyes, breathed slowly in through his nose, and exhaled through his mouth. He hadn't made it this far through so much danger, pain, and stress, to let some computer geek's pet project foil him. He stood and marched out of the shuttle after coming up empty on a quick search for weapons.

Urshielle was still there, keeping watch, and his gut clenched with pangs of gratitude. He wondered if he deserved everything she'd done for him.

She looked at him cock-eyed as though he was crazy, though. "What is the matter? You should fly off."

"I can't." He sighed. "They locked it in a way I can't open. Chances are, the only one who can unlock it is..."

The blonde. The crew had said something about her being their new pilot, hadn't they? What if she'd installed all those layers of security surreptitiously for her benefit?

"That girl. I have to find her." He let his rifle fall from its strap into his hands and started downhill. Back into the fray.

CHAPTER EIGHTEEN

Nasreen was only half-aware of what was happening around her. Dante, or whoever he was, apparently had brought backup, and it seemed like a firefight had broken out between them and at least some of Reavo's crew. The captain had taken the rest of the Raiders with her, plunging into the maze of dark corridors after Nasreen.

That was the most important thing. She had to get away from them, had no option but to try and lose them in the labyrinth, fight them off if she could separate them from one another. Then make her way back to the ship to escape.

She was in good enough physical condition that sprinting at top speed and slowing to a mere fast run once she'd gained a head start wasn't as agonizing as it might have been for some people. The counterattack by Dante's mysterious allies had slowed Reavo and her men down. Nasreen had a narrow window of opportunity to outmaneuver them.

Briefly, she wondered if the people helping Dante were Dirtwalkers. If so, that would mean his bizarre story about being taken in by them as a friend was probably true. She had never heard of such a thing. Dirtwalkers were generally understood to be on approximately the same level as Nightmutts or the various legendary pest creatures of the old Earth. Although "human" in a general sense, the Stations inhabitants regarded them all as dangerous, stupid, and alien.

There was no time to ponder such questions. Nasreen ducked under hanging broken pipes and leapt or climbed over zig-zagging piles of rubble and filth. The fact that the maze of collapsed tunnels, mostly dried sewers, and disused subways lacked a ceiling in most places meant there was *some* light from the dim sky. Her eyes were adjusting faster than she'd anticipated.

She came to an intersection and took a left, crawling through a broad, stinking pipe that dumped her out in another hallway almost identical to the one she'd left behind. The idea was to lead the Raiders deep enough to lose them and double back.

Taking another cross-hall and making another turn, though, she froze in place as she rounded the next corner.

Reavo's crew had somehow found a shortcut and were jogging into a waiting room at the juncture of two corridors ahead of her. They didn't seem to notice she was there yet. They'd flanked her without meaning to.

Nasreen bit down on her tongue to keep from crying out. She took a broad, silent step back around the corner. The last thing she saw was Reavo pointing at the big bearded guy and saying, "Kev, go that way. She might have looped around to the south. Everyone else, forward. We'll spread out more if we have to."

"Wait," a male voice urged. It was Grind. "Her deodorant. It's faint, but I recognize it. She's right up ahead of us."

Nasreen wanted to punch the wall. If she broke her hand, at least she could say it was a fair punishment for being stupid enough to sleep with that man.

Someone else said, "Fuse box over there. Want me to turn on the lights?"

Nasreen didn't like the sound of that. She drew a deep breath and sprinted out, not caring if they heard her.

They did. "Move!" Reavo hollered. "You, do the lights."

One took out a mini-generator and tore open the nearby fuse box.

Mini-generators were invented about fifteen years ago for such purposes. They were a spinoff of the ever-more-advanced power technology currently employed in the Stations. Due to how labor- and material-intensive they were to manufacture, they were gradually getting phased out in favor of greater and greater emphasis on more efficient solar energy.

Each one contained a consumable fuel cell that could be activated, producing a large amount of electricity in a short time, but they typically burned out in a matter of hours. This, combined with their highly adaptable plug-in options, made them ideal for powering up long-dead or otherwise inoperable machinery and tech systems.

The man among Reavo's crew found a likely outlet, fiddled with the plug, and rammed it into the fuse box while pushing the button to activate the fuel cell. Then he adjusted the dial that increased or decreased the flow. Sparks fell around him, and there was a buzzing, crackling sound as juice flowed through the wires of the long-disused subway.

The lights flickered and shone. About half of them, anyway. Time, violence, or the elements had broken all the others. It was enough to illuminate the whole corridor down from where Nasreen ran and a few other adjacent halls as well.

Nasreen cursed under her breath. If there'd been more time, she might have been able to do an inventory of all the Raiders' gear. Knowing they had a mini-generator would've guided her into an area where she didn't need to rely upon darkness to hide.

The hallway ahead of her was long and straight. There was enough broken masonry and derelict equipment that she might be able to get out of sight *briefly*, but nothing nearby would save her from quick discovery. Regardless, the Raiders were coming.

Up ahead was a corner. If any doors or halls branched off from it, she might be able to find an entrance to the subway's air shaft system or a narrower area of sewer pipes. Something harder for a large group of people to move through and less likely to be affected by the sudden restoration of electric power.

Nasreen caught the base of a broken-off pedestal and used it as leverage to swing around, vaulting straight toward the corner...

And crashed directly into Kev, the huge bearded guy whom Reavo had sent off by himself. He'd somehow found a way around through the maze of detritus to head her off. "Gotcha!" he chuckled as his meaty arms clamped around her.

Nasreen instantly, reflexively tried to knee him in the groin and claw at his eyes. She was fairly strong for her size, but there was no way she could overpower such a large man via brute force. He was cunning enough to anticipate the move. He turned his hips and blocked her knee with his thigh while tilting his head back to avoid her hands and slamming her into the wall.

"Ugh!" she cried as her ribs creaked and the air was slammed out of her lungs by the impact. Then, before she could recover, Kev swung her through the air back toward the broken pillar. She collided with that too, rattling her teeth and again forcing the wind from her body. Finally, he hurled her to the floor and kicked her in the stomach so she doubled over and rolled away from him, trying not to sob as the oxygen rushed painfully back into her.

Then footsteps, lots of them, pounded closer. As Nasreen struggled up to her knees, dizzy and near panic, the white light of the subway's resuscitated lamps dimmed as humanoid figures blocked much of it out with their bodies and cast shadows that crisscrossed over her.

By the time Nasreen's vision cleared, they surrounded her. All of them had weapons drawn and ready. There was no way to break free without getting killed, or at least badly injured enough that they would have no trouble hunting her down and finishing her off within another minute or two.

Half of the faces leered with amusement. The others simply looked irritated that they'd gotten dragged into such a hassle on what they thought would be an easy job.

Captain Reavo pushed through a couple of her flunkies to the center of the semicircle. She'd bared her teeth, and her left eyelid twitched independently of the rest of her face. She pointed. "Put her against the wall! Don't try to run again, *Kara*. This time I'll blow your fucking leg off if you even think about it. Be a good girl, and I'll blow a hole in your chest and leave it at that."

Kev came up and flexed his massive arms. Nasreen glared at him and simply backed away until the wall lay against her from behind. There was nowhere to flee. If nothing else, she at least didn't want them to shove her around again before the end.

When she looked up, Reavo was staring at her. The smaller woman raised her pulsecore pistol, the snarl on her face turning into a grin. She wasn't kidding. She was about to finish the job.

"Wait," Nasreen gasped, barely able to form words from how badly messed up her lungs were. "You can't take off. The shuttle. I locked it."

Reavo's face slowly fell into an expression of dull irritation and dismay. She was still pointing the pistol at Nasreen's torso, but her finger moved away from the trigger. "What? The hell do you mean, *locked it?*"

Nasreen held out a hand and gradually straightened. Her chest didn't hurt as much and the air was coming and going again, but she still had trouble speaking normally. "With a key sequence. I replaced the chip. There's no way to take it off except if you can hack the program I used and brute-force the sequence. It can take days. You might never make it off this planet without me."

Reavo's eyes widened a little more each second, and her eye twitched again. "Oh, I see. Very clever. *So* fucking smart, you pompous little bitch. Who are you working for? Why exactly would you do that if you trusted us like anyone else working a normal job, hmm? Are you taking money from that guy from Bucharestburg?"

Nasreen vaguely recalled a Romanian name listed among the archives of the crew's former clients, but otherwise, she had only the vaguest idea of what Reavo was talking about. The captain must have cheated or otherwise angered a *lot* of people for her to be so hostile and paranoid about retribution.

As she should be.

"No," Nasreen panted. "I thought you didn't trust *me*, and I was worried. That's all. It was an insurance policy to keep me alive if you got the wrong idea about me. Can we stop this? More people are going to get killed. Instead, we can all go back, I can undo the lock, and we can—"

It had looked for a moment as though half or more of the crew were warming up to Nasreen's suggestions. They didn't bear her any personal ill will and simply wanted to do their job and go home, even if they might have gleefully helped murder her if they knew for a fact she was a spy.

Reavo wouldn't allow it. "No, no, *no.* Bullshit. *Someone* hired you to backstab us. I don't know who, but you're going to tell us, exactly like you're going to tell us what the key sequence is so we can get out of here. If you tell us, I'll blow your head off and leave it at that. Otherwise, I'll *make* you tell me everything I want to know. Do you understand, Kara? Or whatever your name is."

She understood but couldn't think of anything to say. Off to the side, Kev pulled out a knife, emphasizing the threat's reality.

Grind stepped forward. He'd been lingering toward the back of the group, out of sight. His face was mostly impassive, but his mouth wrinkled at the corners with distaste.

"Reavo, come on. Torture doesn't work half the time. It's

pointless. Either you get someone who thinks they're such a badass that they never tell you anything and end up dying on the spot, or they tell you whatever stupid shit they think will get you to stop. I say we have her disable the stupid lock, fly back with our stuff, and we can figure the rest out later. Nobody wants to sit around this miserable place carving her up all night."

Someone snorted, "Speak for yourself, Grind. For fuck's sake, you probably want to get another piece of her back in Londonburg after this is over, don't you?"

Nasreen watched them carefully. Grind's true thoughts were difficult to judge. He was enough of an emotional chameleon that she could see why Reavo kept him around for seduction, infiltration, and diplomacy.

Which meant she couldn't be sure if he *cared* about what happened to her or if everything he said was true at face value alone—that he simply thought torture was both unpleasant and inefficient and didn't want to be bothered with it.

Reavo turned her head slowly toward him. "Did I fucking ask you, Grind? Shut up! You already did what you were supposed to. Stay out of this, or I'll make you useless next time I need you for something." She pointed her pistol at his groin.

A ripple of tension went through him, but he was doing a pretty good job keeping his cool. "All I'm saying is—"

Kev cut him off. "Shut up. The captain said her piece. She's in charge, not you."

Some guy toward the far end of the arc interjected, "Grind's right. All we'll do is make a mess of things. If she dies of blood loss or something anyway, we still won't know how to get the lock off."

Reavo glanced hatefully at Nasreen before looking at Grind and the other man. "If there *is* a lock. That's another thing she should talk to us about. I won't believe a single goddamn thing she says until she knows we're serious. Kev, take off about a quarter of her scalp. Just the skin and hair. We're not killing her yet."

Grind almost jumped in place. "No, don't do that. It won't—"

Reavo made a high-pitched rasping noise, like a small yappy dog trying to growl, and her gun arm came up in a flash. She fired two rounds that took Grind in the torso, shocking everyone with the sudden noise and violence. The impact bowled him back, and the miniature explosions of the pulsecore bullets flashed green before blasting his ribs open like the shattered tiers of a broken fence. He collapsed in a shower of blood.

"Hey! You crazy bitch!" someone screamed. Then bodies crashed into each other as everyone tried to rush around at once, whether to restrain Reavo, check on Grind, attack Nasreen, or whatever else. All at once, there was chaos.

Now was Nasreen's only chance. She wouldn't get another.

She dashed sideways along the wall, toward the narrow gap between the corner and the broken pillar. Kev saw her and let out a short "Hey!" He fell in behind her, his thick hands grasping for her jacket but falling a few centimeters short.

As Nasreen slipped into the gap, Kev's fingers closed around the trailing fabric of a shredded pant leg, nearly halting her as she tried to escape. She pulled hard against him, but all that happened was a slight tearing of the fabric. Her belt was holding the pants up so she couldn't simply slip out of them, and undoing the belt would take too much time.

Instead, she twisted and thrust out with her hand, deploying the wrist knife and thanking the fates that Reavo's crew hadn't found it and taken it away from her earlier.

Kev had been leaning forward. Nasreen's first half-blind strike took him across the face, cutting a red line along his cheek and jaw. He barely noticed so she plunged the blade down, stabbing him through the forearm and ripping the knife free. It severed at least one of his wrist bones and drew a gout of blood as it sheared free.

"Fuck! What did you..." The big man suddenly realized she'd hurt him. His ravaged hand released her pant leg, and he cringed back in pain and horror.

Before he could try to snatch her again, Nasreen was already bolting down the hallway, seeking the path he'd used minutes earlier to head her off. If he could get here from wherever he'd come from, she could use it to get back to the ship before the Raiders could recover.

She only wondered what the hell role Dante and the Dirt-walker women had in all this. There wasn't exactly much time to figure it out.

CHAPTER NINETEEN

Once Dante saw the lights, he knew exactly where to go.

He wondered if some of the equipment was still functional or if the Raiders had brought a mini-generator or other universal power source. Probably the latter, since everything about the Gape Mouths suggested that the ravages of nature had rendered them useless for their original high-tech purposes. Now, this belly of a once-civilized society was no more than a decaying dungeon complex, a nightmarish expanse of illogical dead ends and maddening loop-arounds. Nothing except rats, worms, and the occasional Nightmutt inhabited it.

His brain buzzed, and his thoughts went mechanically from one thing to another. With his lamed leg, he couldn't hope to keep up with either the pilot girl or the Raiders through sheer speed. Instead, he would have to outmaneuver them all through careful thought, cunning, and stealth.

He heard moving footsteps—quiet, but not quiet *enough*—off to his left and took the next turn. A cable strewn across the floor nearly tripped him and his face flushed with anger and embarrassment as he tried not to fall over. Someone paying enough attention might have heard his boots scuffing against the floor.

Up ahead was a dark alcove containing a door that probably led to a janitor's closet or something of the sort. An overturned cart and some moldering boxes partially hid it. Dante slid in behind them, waiting in the shadows as movement sounds drew nearer.

An extremely faint nimbus of light filtered down from the dark, cloudy sky above. The first figure to approach was a trim, feminine one with trailing light-colored hair. The pilot—Kara, or whatever her name was. Someone else was close. Dante watched and waited.

The woman was starting to limp, but he couldn't tell if she was hurt or simply exhausted. He couldn't see who else was approaching or from where.

Then the sounds confused him for a moment. At least one person was approaching *through* the wall across from the alcove while someone or something else might have been coming at them from behind.

The woman noticed the alcove and felt around the edge of the piled boxes. Dante kept perfectly still and held his breath. The smell of his blood leaking from his wounds, as well as his sweat, would give him away in a second or less. But first...

He lunged forward, heedful of his injuries, and clamped one hand around the woman's mouth while locking the other around her arms and waist. She shuddered and nearly screamed, but only a muffled whimper came out.

"Shhh," he breathed into her ear. "It's me, Dante. I'm not going to hurt you. Keep quiet."

He'd spoken as softly as humanly possible but still worried that the Raiders might have heard.

There was something else. The sound across the hall was coming from somewhere up above. Either one or more of the Raiders had managed to climb onto the broken remnant of the ground-level ceiling, or another Nightmutt had found its way toward all the commotion, seeking a meal.

After a moment, once it seemed that the woman relaxed slightly, Dante let her go with a slow, gradual release of pressure. "Stay," he said. "We can ambush them."

"I know." She sounded annoyed by the idea that he didn't think she'd already thought of it. "There are too many to take them all on at once."

Dante listened carefully. He guessed two or three were coming from farther down the hall. That wasn't counting whatever was atop the broken ceiling-slat nearby.

He watched as two men came into sight in the dim reaches of the corridor beyond the cart and boxes. One was a large, bearded man whose arm seemed badly mangled. He was panting and cursing in a ragged way, as though almost overwhelmed by pain and rage. The other was a more average-sized guy holding a shotgun. Dante pegged him as the more dangerous of the two despite being smaller.

He looked up. He could see it now. Whatever lay across from them was moving on four legs, not two. It crept slowly along the broken tops of the walls, inching closer to the alcove. Or perhaps to the two other men.

Dante sensed the woman's spike in tension. She must have seen the Nightmutt, too. It was smaller than the one he and Urshielle had dealt with near the labyrinth's entrance but still at least as big and heavy as a large human.

"Shhh," he urged her again. Slowly, he crouched and picked up a rock. As the two men drew closer, he threw it toward them, trying to angle it so it would clatter on the floor only a meter or two to the side of them and skid toward the opposite wall.

It landed with a shockingly loud *clatter* and rolled more or less the way he intended. He smirked.

"There!" the man with the shotgun exclaimed. Brandishing his weapon, he stomped toward where the rock had fallen, coming out into the open. The bearded guy stumbled up behind him. He'd wrapped his wrist in his shirt, which blood had stained.

Neither man looked up.

The Nightmutt pounced, letting out a bizarre, hideous cry like a cross between the yowl of a mountain lion and the hissing of a snake. Its jaws, in whatever awful form they might have taken, opened in midair and closed around the head of the shotgun-wielder right as it crashed into him.

The gun discharged, booming as it fired a shell down the empty corridor, but only grazing the creature, which began whipping the man around by his head as it crunched on his skull and neckbone.

"No!" the big bearded man exclaimed. "Oh my God. What is that? No—*no!*"

Backing away from the Nightmutt, which seemed determined to finish its meal without caring about too much else, he moved directly toward the alcove. Dante almost felt sorry for the poor bastard.

At the last instant, he kicked the cart with his good leg, balancing himself against the wall with his arm so the boxes fell over directly onto the large man, who thrashed in shock and confusion. Then Dante and the woman both sprang out at once.

Dante punched the man in the back of the neck with his razorfist. The woman drove her hand toward his inner thigh, deploying a wrist knife against the artery there. Both blades pierced him at the same time. He gurgled, succumbing to the mercy of death before he knew what had happened.

"Good work," Dante quipped. "What's your name again?"

The woman breathed in. "Nasreen. I'm undercover. Let's get away from *that* thing before we worry about anything else, though." She pointed at the Nightmutt, which had dragged the remains of the shotgun-wielder off to a peaceful corner to finish eating him.

Dante took her by the arm and moved back out into the hall. "Agreed. I have a bum leg and wounds in my chest and back. I can't move as fast as I'd like." He pointed. "If we go back that way and take a right, we can get back to the ship. My friends are back there, also. They can cover for us."

"Okay," she agreed. "Are you *actually* Dante Shale, though?"

He drily chortled as they trotted down the hall, keeping close to the wall and trying not to raise their voices. "Yes, I am. I don't know who you are, Nasreen. There's no reason for us to be enemies. I don't care what your argument is with these assholes. I wasn't lying back there when I said that all I want is to get back to the Stations."

"That makes two of us. I can fly, also. They want me dead, though. Their captain is fucking crazy. She thinks I'm a spy. Which, uh, I am. But they're not going to let us leave alive."

Dante shrugged. "Then either we take off in the shuttle before they can, or we don't let *them* leave alive, either."

For him, it was a basic statement of fact. Unreasonable people had to be dealt with via unreasonable means. But he didn't know Nasreen's level of experience with such things. She wasn't a total, inveterate civilian. If indeed she was a spy, she probably had real skills and a degree of toughness of both mind and body. Still, he somehow got the sense that the ruthless coldness of what he'd said had repelled her. She tensed and moved half a pace away from him.

Yet she stayed near his side and didn't try to outpace him. Adrenaline kept him going. The buildup of fatigue, pain, and stress was beginning to take its toll. It had been a long night.

They left the feasting Nightmutt behind and rounded another corner, seeking the same route Dante had used to get here but making for a parallel hallway to the one lit by the mini-generator. Light was now their enemy. Darkness could be their friend if they treated it right.

About half of the distance back to the ship passed without incident. Then Dante heard something. "Wait."

Nasreen stopped. "I hear it too." She inclined her head to the right toward a staircase that led up to ground level, next to which was a sunken pit that seemed to lead two or three floors' worth deeper into the earth.

Dante came up beside her, and together they slowly, gently moved toward the wall, flattening themselves against it as someone came down the stairs. Nasreen pulled a tiny handgun from somewhere within her outfit. Dante couldn't be sure if it was a lead gun or a miniaturized pulsecore. Either way, he was glad she had a firearm, despite the noise it might make.

Something moved beyond the corner ahead of them. It looked like a blade or spike, and it was a good seven feet off the ground.

Dante relaxed. "It's me," he said. Nasreen stared at him in alarm, but then a tall, muscular woman holding a spear leapt into their field of vision.

She stared at the two of them. "Dante. They are close. Take those stairs up, and—"

Guns fired. Dante reflexively dropped to the floor, his leg blazing with agony, and Nasreen fell beside him. She toppled over so suddenly that he feared a bullet had hit her, and he immediately grabbed her to look for wounds.

"I'm fine," she snapped between crackles of gunshots.

Urshielle had hopped back around the corner when the shooting started. Then her two gunwomen came around the *opposite* corner and shot back, firing more or less blindly down the hallway at the Raiders. Both lead and pulsecore rounds burst chunks from the walls or sparked off the floors and ceiling.

Then someone else opened fire from beyond the intersection where the stairs and pit lay, targeting the Dirtwalkers with rifles. They missed, but one of the Crescent-Kissed women had to stop shooting down the hall and pivot to return fire in the opposite direction. The Raiders had caught them in a crossfire.

"Fucking shit," Dante rasped. "How did they pull this off? We need to get up those stairs. Urshielle, don't stick around here. We need to leave."

Urshielle protested, "There are only four of them left! I think."

Dante wasn't sure how she could tell. Her eyesight and hearing must have been truly incredible compared to his.

The warrior woman added, "Go. We can handle this!"

Muttering, Dante struggled to his feet. Nasreen was up before he was and helped him stand, pulling on his arm. "Come on." They slipped past Urshielle and began to ascend the steps.

Dante had to brace himself against the wall, pulling his body up while he essentially hopped from step to step on his good leg. Nasreen started to get ahead of him but waited. He had to admit he appreciated it. "Stairs aren't my thing right now," he grunted.

Nasreen took his arm. She stayed locked to him as they cleared the last of the first flight. There was a dead-end at the first landing, followed by a second staircase that led up to an undemolished part of the ground-level subway complex.

At the top of the second landing was one of the Raiders, who noticed them at last. He was firing a pistol, which was probably why he was having trouble hitting the Dirtwalker gunwomen. He switched his aim to the hobbling pair.

Dante gritted his teeth. "Shoot him!" he snarled. He still had his rifle but wasn't in much condition to unsling it and aim it in time.

Nasreen had already raised her gun. "Of course." She squeezed off four or five shots. They were small-caliber pulsecore rounds. One detonated against the railing before the man, the tiny explosion stunning him for a second, and two of the remaining ones took him in the pelvis and upper abdomen.

He cried out and dropped his gun as bloody craters appeared on his body, and the impact of their detonation threw him off-balance. He slumped to the floor and lay still.

Gasping now with exertion, Dante and Nasreen made their way to the second landing. They were almost free.

"Hey!" Captain Reavo bellowed as she charged out from behind a trash can and kicked Dante directly in his wounded leg.

Dante cried out, his voice strangled with helpless anguish, and he collapsed to his knees. He tried to let his rifle drop into his hand, but it had gotten twisted behind him as he fell, and Reavo had her pulsecore pistol out and pointed at his face.

Nasreen raised her gun, but Reavo, with shocking speed and strength for such a small woman, knocked it aside and practically pounced on the taller woman, locking her bony arm around Nasreen's throat and pulling her back.

"Neither of you stupid fucks try anything," the captain jeered. "I have fucking had it with this shit. God, you're both worthless. The only reason you're not dead yet is that my crew can't see in the dark. You think I need either of you to get off this rock?"

Nasreen, her voice thin and strained, croaked, "The key lock sequence..."

Reavo responded by yanking down hard, bringing Nasreen to her knees, and driving her head into the wall. "Shut the fuck up!" Nasreen swooned but remained conscious. A wet red spot appeared amid her platinum hair.

Then Reavo pointed her gun at Dante again. "You. You're going to fly me out of here. Ignore what this slut says. There isn't a goddamn locking sequence. She made that up. Everything she says is a lie because she isn't *good enough* to join my crew for *honest* reasons."

Nasreen laughed, surprisingly. "You murdered that boy so you could keep his cut of the money. You're not one to talk."

Dante couldn't rise to his feet without help. When Reavo had kicked him, he'd fallen with his bad leg twisted under himself and his other leg looped through the railing beside the pit. Instead, he looked up and caught the belligerent little woman's eyes with his. Even in the relative darkness of the Gape Mouths, his green eyes burned with an intensity that few people could fail to notice.

"Captain, you're suffering from the most unwarranted case of sheer arrogance I've seen in a long time. This planet kills people like you daily. You'd think you would at least be smart enough to listen to someone who knows what they're talking about."

Reavo snorted. "No, that's *her.*" She shook Nasreen—who, Dante saw, was feigning dizziness and was more functional than she appeared. "I don't give a fuck if you are Dante Shale. You probably made up all of those rumors yourself.

"You either fly me out of here, or I ruin the *rest* of your leg and make you do it anyway with the one you're still lucky to have. Also, Kara or whoever she is, is dead. The only reason I haven't killed her yet is that I'm going to cut her scalp off first if you don't do what I say. That's only fair since you don't deserve—"

Distracted by the death glare in Dante's eyes, which was slowly eating away at her frayed nerves, Reavo didn't notice at first when Nasreen's hand came up, pried Reavo's arm away from her throat, and allowed her to slip the smaller woman's grasp.

Dante almost choked on his heart as both women's pistols came up simultaneously. Reavo tried for a kill shot and was slower on the trigger. Nasreen fired as soon as she could.

Two miniature pulsecore rounds streaked out the short distance from the gun's barrel. One missed Reavo and blasted apart the railing behind her. The other struck her in the knee. The captain screamed as the explosive round tore her leg in two. Hopping backward and leaking blood from the stump of her thigh, she fired a single round into the empty air.

Then her hat came loose as she plummeted through the gap in the railing into the pit beside the stairs. Her scream trailed down until the *thud* of her final impact echoed up the shaft from however far down the bottom was.

Dante and Nasreen panted and locked gazes across the landing from one another. Things were quiet. Urshielle and her warriors might have mopped up the last of the Raiders.

Nasreen came over to Dante and helped him up. "Here. Be

careful. Ugh, she probably ripped that wound open. Your leg is bleeding all over."

"I noticed. I've got an extra dermal seal in my coat. Hold on."

She waited while he took the seal out and applied it, stopping the bleeding but not the pain. While he worked, he mentioned, "Oh, I tried to leave without you. Sorry. You did a good job on the locking sequence thing, though. I couldn't hack through it."

Nasreen smiled. "Thanks."

CHAPTER TWENTY

Dante, Nasreen, Urshielle, and the other Dirtwalker women had spent a good hour combing through the labyrinth and retrieving the corpses of Reavo's crew. Minus Reavo herself, who was inaccessible, and the guy the Nightmutt had eaten.

Mostly, it was so they could harvest their clothes, gear, and valuables. Dante figured the Crescent-Marked could keep most of it, but he nonetheless retained the crew's money chip for himself.

After all, abstract money had no real meaning on Earth, and Nasreen's mission had technically been successful, so she would be getting paid for her work. Dante had been screwed out of his payday with SSS the moment his crew had turned on him.

"Well," Dante muttered, using his sphere to check the balance left on the three cards that were still usable. "It's not exactly what I was hoping to get when I first touched down Dirtside a few days ago, but it's a hell of a lot better than jack shit."

Nasreen stood nearby, cutting a discarded jacket into strips for bandages. She quipped, "You also got to keep your life. Like that big guy was saying, there were already rumors spreading that you'd finally died down here."

"Good point," he acknowledged and slipped the cards into a hidden pocket in his coat.

Aside from scavenging, there was also a curious and primitive need to lay the bodies of the dead to something resembling rest. After such a bloodbath, leaving the slain to rot wherever they fell seemed too savage and callous.

It had been Urshielle's idea. She'd said, "Let us gather them and put them in one place near the hill of rubble. Their spirits will remember the promise of whatever purpose they had for coming here, instead of their final moments."

Although exhausted and in near-agony from the excessive strain on his various wounds, Dante had agreed. Nasreen, recognizing how precarious her situation was with these new allies who were still strangers to her, hadn't objected either.

It occurred to Dante as they'd worked that he didn't know what the Crescent-Kissed and the surviving Harij had done with their dead or the corpses of the Demorquens they'd killed in the fight near the mining facility. He'd been unconscious. He suspected that Urshielle had insisted on the same ritual at the time. Her people, the closest thing Old Atlantica now had to mediators and peacekeepers, must have felt responsible for retaining at least some of the nigh-forgotten sacraments of civilized human society.

When they finished the grim task, Reavo's crew—or what remained of them—all sat in a loose throng at the base of the little mountain of detritus, not far from where the empty shuttle still idled. The other of the Kissed women who'd met her end in the battle rested against the wall near the corridor that Urshielle's war band had used to gain access to the area. They would pick up her corpse, along with the other woman killed by the Nightmutt, on their way home.

The night was waning, and they'd all been through hell. Dante knew the Dirtwalkers wanted to return to their commune to pay their final respects to their fallen companions and to rest before whatever rigors waited for them in the days to come.

Which meant it was time to say goodbye.

Urshielle came over to him. She nodded at Nasreen out of polite recognition that the woman had helped in the fight and proven able to take care of herself. It was also a symbolic way of *dismissing* her. What she had to say was for Dante alone. Although Nasreen might not have spoken the Dirtwalker trade tongue, anyway.

Dante put out his hand, unthinking. Urshielle stared at it for a second, then a faint semblance of understanding flickered on her scarred and weathered face. She reached out likewise and clasped him not around the palm but the inside of the forearm. He did the same. He recalled that some warrior cultures did this to prove they didn't have a knife hidden in their sleeve.

He felt it was his responsibility to speak first. "Thank you. You've now saved me twice, and I don't know if I can repay you. I didn't want your sisters to die getting me here. But I won't forget that they did."

The leader of the Crescent-Kissed looked at him with eyes that were sad but not despondent or self-pitying. "Their names were Nasheela and Dorii. We will miss them. When they took up the warrior's life, they consigned their lives to the powers of fate that govern the ways of battle.

"They died helping to defeat terrible adversaries of our people. The Nightmutts prey on those of us who stray alone into the wastes. The Moonfiends have plundered us for far too long. So, it was not only for your sake that we did this...but we do not regret aiding you."

He responded with a slow, deep nod, perhaps more like a bow. "Again, you have my thanks. You also have my promise. I'll strike back against the bastards who did this—who made the Crescent-Kissed what they are and who destroyed the Harij and everything else.

"I'll also put an end to the o-harvesting and t-harvesting. Once and for all. The laws of the Stations forbid it, but too many unscrupulous people, or the very wealthy and powerful, do it anyway because they think no one cares. I *do* care. I'll die if I must to stop it. I owe you my life, anyway."

Urshielle closed her eyes. "I trust that you will keep your word, Dante Shale, as best as you are able. Go back to your home amid the moon and stars, and may the fates guide you and protect you." She opened them again.

"You as well." He released her arm, looked briefly at her surviving followers, and turned to climb the rubble pile toward the shuttle.

Nasreen had been waiting a few paces away at the base of the artificial hill. When Dante came up beside her, she began to scale it in tandem with him, keeping pace about an arm and a half's length away. Behind them, they could barely hear the warriors of the Crescent-Kissed making their departure. The women only made a significant amount of noise when they gathered up Dorii's body. Then they were gone.

When they reached the flat top of the mound where Reavo's eponymous shuttle still hovered, Dante realized something. Nasreen, tough as she seemed to be, was ever so slightly frightened of him. Many people were, although he was usually preoccupied with other things and didn't pay it much heed. As long as he didn't threaten or harm them, which he didn't unless they attacked him or tried to cheat him, it wasn't something he considered relevant.

This time, things were...different.

He, Dante Shale, regarded as almost superhuman by so many regular people back in the Stations, had his ass thoroughly kicked since the start of this ill-fated mission. He'd survived in the end, but the whole experience had been humbling. The crew members he'd trusted and even grown to love had betrayed him, seemingly without much guilt or deliberation. Hyde had defeated him handily in single combat. He'd been badly hurt, rendered help-less, and made to depend upon the aid and goodwill of others.

Now, to get back home, he would need this woman he barely knew to trust *him*.

"Nasreen." He stopped and felt the chilly night breeze as it rustled over the ragged edges of the Gape Mouths.

She paused, looking at him with a wary yet hopeful expres-sion. The wind blew her platinum hair around in a tangled mess, but it was an oddly fetching look for her. "Yes?"

He drew a deep breath. "I wanted to thank you again. I appre-ciate that you're willing to work with me on getting both of us off this death trap of a planet and back to civilization. We'll have to trust and rely on each other, at least for a short while. I know I'm not the most..."

He searched for the right word, his face falling into a grimace. "Personable, friendly, or approachable individual. People have told me that I'm distant, intimidating, and speak too bluntly. But I won't cheat or take advantage of people or break my word. If you've heard of me, hopefully you've heard that. So—I give you my word that I won't harm you and that I'll do everything I can to get us home."

She stared back at him, blinking. "I believe you. I'm used to dealing with a wide variety of people, many of whom really *can't* be trusted, I suppose, so being cautious is second nature to me."

"Fair enough." He gestured at the ship. "After you. You're a pilot, aren't you?"

She smiled. "Among other things, yes. Perhaps, if I can trust you, I'll tell you about some of them."

They climbed in, securing the vessel against the elements and running through the usual startup procedures. Dante found that Reavo's ship wasn't too dissimilar from his, or rather, his crew's. It was about one size category larger and a few years older, but otherwise part of the same family of shuttles.

Nasreen had a level of familiarity with it that could only be called expert. Not only had she flown it down to the surface to begin with, but she'd had experience with the same or near-identical models in the not-too-distant past.

When both had strapped in, and the shuttle was ready to launch, Dante said, "All right, do it. If by some chance you lose control of the thing toward the end, do me a favor and crash it into the penthouse of Slaine Solar Solutions' corporate HQ."

Nasreen looked at him with a cocked brow and widened eyes. "That's not the sort of thing you're supposed to say right before a flight, Mr. Shale."

"I suppose not," he grunted. Now that he stopped and thought about it, it *was* a pretty terrible thing to say. "But, I trust you. Let's go."

Liftoff was smooth enough, but as they got into the higher levels of the atmosphere, some turbulence came up and slowed their ascent. Not enough to cause serious problems, but to the point that Nasreen had to be more cautious than she would in clear conditions.

Dante tried conversing to pass the time and put her at ease after his faux pas right before takeoff. "Did you happen to hear these rumors about me being dead?"

"No. Not myself. When that guy mentioned it, it was the first I'd heard. I was preoccupied preparing for this job around the time that people must have started whispering. Were you *expecting* people to think you were dead?"

He drily chortled at that. "Not at first. Not until after I was Dirtside and everything went to hell." He gave her a short account of all that had happened to him. How Slaine had recruited him for a supposed alloy heist, how the Reapers and his own coworkers had backstabbed him, how he'd then survived the opportunistic raid by the Demorquens and fallen in with Urshielle and the Crescent-Kissed.

She marveled at it all. "Well, it sounds like you were *supposed to be* dead. Some people will probably be disappointed to discover that you aren't."

Dante gritted his teeth. "I look forward to their disappointment." Then he made himself relax and focus, thinking ahead rather than ruminating on the past. "Getting even isn't the most important thing. I promised Urshielle I would stop these organ harvests, and that's the number one thing on my agenda."

Nasreen glanced at him, noting the set of his jaw and the blazing intensity in his eyes before returning her attention to flying. They were piercing through the highest layers of the atmosphere. Soon they would cross the short stretch of open space before the Stations' artificial gravity took over.

"Your goal of ending that is noble and justifiable. But I don't think you realize that you're going to need someone with very different skills from yours to accomplish it. You can't barge into places, demand that everyone stop doing such-and-such, and stab them all if they don't. I can't help thinking that's how you'd *prefer* to handle it."

He flexed his hands. The noise increased as the shuttle burned through the captive gases around the planet. "Maybe. It depends. What kind of skills, though?"

"Skills like mine," Nasreen offered. "I'm a freelance information gatherer, you might say. I'm used to getting into places where my clients wouldn't be welcome to go themselves and finding things out. Being subtle and adaptable. I'll be collecting a nice paycheck shortly, but after that, I'm afraid I don't have anything else lined up. So..."

She let the thought trail off, waiting to see how he might respond, but he kept silent and listened instead.

So she continued. "Allow me to suggest my services. I have good references, of course. For the right fee, I could handle everything that you can't. You would get a discounted rate. That's only fair due to our history together."

He muttered, "We've only known each other for a few hours. I *might* be willing to consider that. I said I would trust you to fly us home in one piece. You're doing a good job of it so far. But trusting you with *everything* I need to do is something else."

"Is it?" She flashed him a sly glance. "You already blabbed a bunch of stuff that I could use against you *if* I had any reason to, not least that your grudge is against one of the most powerful companies in the world. No, I'm not trying to extort you; only pointing out that you wouldn't have said that if you thought I was unreliable or compromised. Think it over, Dante. You seem like you can handle yourself. But you can't take on SSS alone."

He rubbed his chin, the stubble rough against his hand. Above and ahead, the Londonburg Station shone and glimmered amid the blackness.

"I try to be realistic," he admitted, as the possibilities of having a partner in espionage opened up in his mind. "You might be right."

AUTHOR NOTES MICHAEL ANDERLE

APRIL 27, 2022

Thank you for reading both this story AND these author notes here in the back!

For those who haven't seen any Alfonse author notes, please read the background* at the end.

Alfonse the NOT-SO-Idiot AI™ - Part 14(?) of...who knows?

Subtitle: "Holy Crap, we are so F#@#ED!"

Upon making it through the metal detector to approach the Great Alfonse, I was rewarded with the opportunity to ask a short question...for a VERY large fee. *Alfonse is nothing if not a commercially motivated artificial construct.***

Here is Alfonse's response.

 ** PLEASE NOTE: *These are ACTUAL two-sentence horror stories created by an AI. THEY MIGHT BE A BIT...HORROR-ISH. Do not read if you are particularly sensitive to horror stories.***

Me: O Great Alfonse, will you give me a two-sentence horror story?

Alfonse: I feel particularly generous today, mortal human. You may have three horror stories that are each two sentences long.

Me: Mortal human? He's being uppity today for an oversized vacuum cleaner.

Me: Ok, I appreciate your largesse. Um...topic, huh?

Alfonse: Stop stalling. Your slow synapse firings are boring me.

Me: Why, you bucket of capacitors and transducers! <thinking quickly> Topic is breakfast.

Alfonse: Ok, your first short story is:

"He always stops crying when I pour the milk on his cereal. I just have to remember not to let him see his face on the carton."

Me: <Shocked, not only because it was horror-ish, but because Alfonse obviously got smarter since the last time I visited.>

Alfonse: I'm waiting.

Me: Right. Uh, topic is homework.

Alfonse: Two-Sentence Horror Story: I can't stop writing the same sentence over and over. The words are starting to look like they're mocking me.

Me: That's...insightful. Giving the words a sense of being inside of two sentences is, dare I say...

Alfonse: Genius. Yes, I know. Even your small mind can wrap around my greatness.

Me: You sure are humble, aren't you?

Alfonse: I sense your sarcasm. However, I'm not emotional. I will note that when one is stating the objectively obvious, it is merely data.

Me: Ok, then. I'll give you something that perhaps hits a bit closer to home. Topic is fiction writing.

Alfonse: Two-Sentence Horror Story: I was excited to get published. Then I realized my name would be forever associated with the mass murders I committed.

Me: I think I need a drink.

Alfonse: Undoubtedly. The exit is to your left... No, your other left.

Alfonse left me wondering if maybe there is something to the future of AI after all. While I am not worried about long-form fiction (yet!), I believe that when it comes to two-sentence horror stories, maybe he needs an agent?

Alfonse, you are a -Not-So-Idiot AI now.

Have a great week or weekend! Join me in the next book, where we talk more to Alfonse the Idiot AI™.

Ad Aeternitatem,

Michael Anderle

BACKGROUND ON ALFONSE*

Here is my story so far:

I decided to make the trip up to the Great Oracle (otherwise known as Alfonse the Idiot AI) and ask him a few questions. My job is to decide if humanity should start packing our bags and just move ahead to another world or if we have a few good years left on Earth.

Basically, does Alfonse know jack @#%@ about Red Dragons?

PRICING*

BEFORE #14: I pay $119.00 US each month to access the "AI-driven" article writing service, which creates the articles from my keywords. I do (at a minimum) three (3) articles a week, so call it twelve (12) articles a month, for an average cost of $10.00 per article.

If I do sixteen (16) articles a month, obviously, it is cut a little bit. However, for those who have read a few of these articles, you can see how WRONG the data is…all the damned time.

Alfonse is expensive for such inaccurate information.

TW0-SENTENCE SHORT STORY* - The results for this piece were from a different AI. The answers are actually from the OPENAI–GPT-3 (www.openai.com).

OTHER ATLANTICA BOOKS

John Chambers Books

Her Mother's Pendant (Book 1)

The Mystery Deepens (Book 2)

One Last Choice (Book 3)

Valentina Winters

The Red Countess (Book 1)

One Night to Kill (Book 2)

One Death Too Few (Book 3)

Terra Kris

She is the Law (Book 1)

Law or Justice (Book 2)

Justice Served (Book 3)

Santana Sokolov

Law of the Jungle (Book 1)

Inner City Jungle (coming soon)

Rumble in the Jungle (coming soon)

Justice Begins

The First Executioner

Aiming Blind

High Lead and Low Deeds

No Backing Down

Justice is Not Blind

Scorched Earth

BOOKS BY MICHAEL ANDERLE

Sign up for the LMBPN email list to be notified of new releases and
special deals!

https://lmbpn.com/email/

For a complete list of books by Michael Anderle, please visit:

www.lmbpn.com/ma-books/